A TAXING PROBLEM

THE PSYCHOLOGIST'S PRESCRIPTION FOR A JUST TAX SYSTEM

DR. MITCH

PAGE PUBLISHING
Conneaut Lake, PA

First originally published by Page Publishing 2022

ISBN 979-8-88654-151-9 (pbk)
ISBN 979-8-88654-153-3 (digital)

Printed in the United States of America

TABLE OF CONTENTS

✧ ✧ ✧

LIST OF TABLES

✧ ✧ ✧

CHAPTER 1

Justification

Anger is a response to pain and fear. It is, what we call in psychology, a secondary emotion, meaning it is a response to a primary emotion. Anger is the emotional response that energizes our actions taken in response to pain and fear. Among our earliest experiences of emotional pain are events or treatment that are perceived as unfair. The most common experiences that cause people pain and result in anger, whether expressed or repressed, are those that ultimately lead to the refrain, "It's not fair!" It's not fair when we are neglected or abused in childhood. It's not fair when our siblings or peers are treated better than we are by our parents or teachers.

Since societal anger is escalating, we can infer that the pain of living in society has been escalating. This pain is the source of political unrest, which is escalating in our country and in the world due to treatment or conditions that are perceived as unfair. This pain fuels the anger that energizes political protest and sometimes political violence. When people have outsized angry reactions, that reaction can be best understood as a present moment triggering through the brain's synaptic connections what I like to call emotional echoes from the past. The fact is that our brain stores the emotional memories of events both remembered, forgotten, and that were forged before we had the capacity for language and narrative creation. Remembered memory is called extrinsic memory, and the well-spring of other emotional memories is called intrinsic memory.

Most of us can recall painful moments from childhood, either from interactions with our parents, siblings, teachers, other kids, or adults when we hurt because we suffered something which we felt was unfair. Most of these times the pain suffered then was not processed with the assistance of a nurturing adult. As a result, the pain of the moment got stored in our limbic brain together with the pains of other similar experiences. This builds up over the years into an emotional memory reservoir. When we experience unfairness in our adult lives, the connectivity of our brains recalls into the present moment painful feelings from that reservoir. Hence, our anger response appears inexplicitly much bigger than the circumstances would appear to warrant. When people relate some big angry reaction, they will often say, "It seems so silly now."

This individual human experience is very important to understand in our current time of political unrest. The relationship between political unrest and emotion is well-known but rarely discussed even in academic circles. There is much discussion of and advocacy for economic or social justice. Much of the discussion, though, seems to miss the point of the nexus to human emotion. What is important is not equality of wealth or other measurable criteria, but rather the perception of fairness.

When any portion of our population experiences that something is unfair about the social, political, or economic systems in our country, or for that matter, the world, it triggers the reservoir of psychic pain carried in the recesses of the minds of our fellows. This reservoir of pain and fear of more pain can be understood as the "it's not fair" wound. As already pointed out, the human response to pain and fear is anger. This perspective explains all political upheavals from the Boston Tea Party to the Vietnam antiwar movement; from the Black Lives Matter Movement to the January 6, 2021, attack on Capitol Hill.

Since taxes are the primary way that the costs of government and its programs and services are financed, this book looks primarily at the unfairness of our systems of taxation, and through that lens, the unfairness in our society. And I propose a solution that I believe we can all get behind because it is rooted in fairness as that is understood. This book will suggest how we, in the great middle-class, can lower our total tax burden and pay off the national debt at the same time by more fairly distributing the necessary burden of paying for the type of society we would choose to have. In doing so, I expect I may suffer ridicule or worse from certain segments of our society. After all, many of our fellows find any change threatening, and radical change, radically threatening. What I am suggesting will seem, to some people, radical change.

I am, as of this writing, seventy-one years old. I am a former attorney and law professor who taught business and property related courses in law school. I studied microeconomics and macroeconomics in university and in law school studied taxation and property. I would hope that my background entitles my views to be taken seriously enough to inspire further study by policy makers and economists. I welcome input from others who think that the approach is flawed or has promise. I can be contacted through email at flatwealthtax@yahoo.com, an email address set up for that purpose.

The violence, injustice, and myopia of so many in power in the world leaves my heart in despair. As Machiavelli in his classic work *The Prince* made clear, it is in the interest of the prince to avoid fomenting rebellion among the governed. Just as individuals overreact to perceived unfairness in our personal lives, as a society we will likely overreact to perceived unfairness in our systems of government and social organization. Putting on my social psychologist hat for a moment, I suggest that the best place to start correcting our social and political unease is by reforming our tax system to one that is fair.

As you take yourself through my chapters, I ask only that you bring honesty and openness to my ideas. And if you see the light that I see, the promise of a better present and a better future for all, I ask of you one thing more. I ask that you find the willingness to play an active role in transmitting these ideas to others and transmuting them into reality in our lives.

CHAPTER 2

Politics, Power, and Control of Resources

This book is about money and morality. I ask you: "If you could live in a world in which you paid no income tax, no sales tax, no real property taxes, no social security taxes, no Medicare taxes, no federal or state disability taxes, no vehicle registration fees, no park fees, no fees or taxes to government of any kind, other than 2% of your *net* worth annually, would you be willing?"

Consider this fact and its import.

In 1789, Ben Franklin wrote these words in a letter to Jean Baptiste Le Roy. "But in this world, nothing can be said to be certain, except death and taxes." How many times in the late twentieth and early twenty-first centuries have we heard spoken some variation of Mr. Franklin's observation?

Unlike "death," though, taxes are purely a human invention. How we tax currently is a detail that we accept largely without question. Yes, we debate and tinker with things like tax rates, mortgage interest deductibility, etc. But no fundamental examination of how we tax is pursued in personal or political discourse.

As children, we are never much conscious of taxation. Oh sure, perhaps we overhear grown-ups complaining about income taxes, sales taxes, or even property taxes. Perhaps we hear talk about sin taxes, consumption taxes, or gas taxes. But the existence of these taxes

4

is "a given." We approach the subject of taxation much like that of geography, as forming an immutable landscape.

Sales tax is the first tax we experience firsthand. Income tax is usually the first substantial tax and the one to which we seem to give most of our attention. When we first start working and earning our own money, we feel the bite of withholding taxes but never really know why they are taken from our earnings. Nor do many of us even ask.

A scholarly sophistication is not needed to understand that taxes are collected by government so that government services can be provided. So when I say we never really inquire as to why we are paying them, I don't mean "why" in that sense.

Police, fire, sanitation, health, transportation, roads, parks, schools, defense are all enterprises that support our well-being and safety. Of course, we must have a way to pay for these things from which we all benefit. But why do we pay income taxes, property taxes, excise taxes, *ad valorem* taxes, sin taxes, etc.? Why do we collect them as we do and not in some other way? One short answer and one which would be accurate is "historical accident." But a better answer is that over time, the tax burden has been allocated through small political decisions made for the benefit of those with political power.

Politics can be understood as society's ongoing discussion about what services should be provided by government to assure a desired quality of life. At a deeper level, politics becomes about answering the question, "How should we allocate among competing interests the resources collected by government?" This is the question answered by the legislative process as we practice it in the United States. But rarely, if ever, has there been any substantive discussion in our living rooms, academic institutions, venues of political discourse, or legislative chambers about how to fairly allocate the burden of paying for the society that we want to enjoy, whatever we collectively decide how that society should look.

Of course, one hears discussion in the news about the merits of this income tax hike, or that reduction, this sales tax hike or a hike on gasoline taxes. Lately we have even heard rumblings of a limited wealth tax on billionaires. We hear about the concepts "regressive taxation" or "progressive taxation" in the context of any tax at issue, and some, I fear relatively few, of our citizens even know what these terms mean.

The public political discourse creates the illusion that we are concerned with fairness in taxation. But we are not really. How do I know? The tax system overall has been and continues to be highly regressive, which is fundamentally unfair. In our systems of taxation, the poor and the middle class heavily subsidize the wealthiest among us. Our tax policies are largely welfare for the rich. The fact is that our elected officials at all levels are driven to almost manic fund-raising activity. It is not surprising, therefore, that the rich have an outsized influence on policy and legislation.

America's Declaration of Independence states, "We hold these truths to be self-evident, that all men are created equal."

The Declaration's statement was brilliant rhetoric offered to justify a revolution against the oppression of a European tradition of inherited aristocracy and colonialism. But, as Confucius observed more than five hundred years before the birth of Christ, "By nature, men are nearly alike; by practice, they get to be wide apart."

As a statement of practical reality, relating either to the time in which it was written or to today, the Declaration's statement is absurd. Why? Lots of reasons.

First, some people are born smarter, stronger, faster, or healthier than others. Then too, one child is born to immigrant parents living from meager paycheck to meager paycheck. Another is born to a crack-whore mother whose need for a fix is more urgent than the needs of her child. One child is born into a middle-class family of nine children; another is born the only child of the granddaughter of John D. Rockefeller. Some are born into families of well-adjusted people who are models of balanced living, and some into families perpetuating the psychological and/or physical brutality of past generations.

In what sense, then, are all men created equal? As a matter of theological ideal, they may be equal before God, but in the practical realities of our lives, they are wide apart. They are not afforded equal opportunity for a good life either by nature, circumstance, or from society.

Society is helpless to alter some of these inequalities. But many of these inequalities are directly the result of society's half-conscious decision to create and protect the right to accumulate wealth, how to do it, and for whose benefit.

When have you heard or participated in discussion of how to use government's need and power to tax to move further toward the idealistic proclamation of our Declaration of Independence, "We hold these truths to be self-evident that all men are created equal"? Anyone can see that it is less a statement of fact than an expression of an ideal, and perhaps a national aspiration. When has anyone in Congress or our president engaged in such a discussion? The time to engage in this discussion is now.

As the forces of destruction and subjugation on our planet spiral out of control, the best hope for mankind is to raise the consciousness of our species, one person at a time. Society and government decisions about how to allocate benefits and costs of social organization could be part of the solution and not part of the problem. The point was implied in Leonardo Di Caprio's clarion call in the documentary film about the environment, "The Eleventh Hour." But even in the context of his grand work, which explored the connections between seemingly disparate facts and the consequences of this connectedness, no one articulated that our decisions about taxation contribute largely to the potentially catastrophic global problems that the film is meant to reveal. And yet they do.

When you think about it, the long-term accumulation of wealth is as contrary to natural law as the idea that the resources of the planet are inexhaustible. Contrary to natural law means contrary to nature. Not that the desire to accumulate wealth is contrary to nature. One only need look to the common tree squirrel to see that, or for that matter, to the beaver, bees, and many other animals. But in nature, because of predation, wealth is never accumulated long term.

I do not mean to leave mankind outside of nature in this discussion. Except for the activities of organized society, such as the building of roads, dams, and schools, the activities of science, industry, and engineering, and the maintenance and enforcement of laws, to name a few, no one would be able to accumulate much in the way of wealth. Social norms, many codified in law, are created, protected, and preserved by human society and society's institutions, the police, the legislature, the judiciary, banks, insurance companies, the military, etc. Without these, no person would be able to accumulate massive amounts of wealth and preserve that wealth for long. Society and its organized institutions are one's only defense against the inevitable pilfering of one's wealth by others that are bigger, stronger, and more ruthless.

Accumulation of wealth, therefore, and likewise the ability to enjoy the benefits of the accumulation and control of wealth is possible only through the availability, protection, and use of the forces that society brings to bear. This idea merits repeating. The "haves" of society possess and enjoy their wealth only because of the use of governmental force founded upon the social compact and the society's creation and maintenance of the infrastructures so necessary for commercial activity of every type.

In a world without social organization, one's capacity to accumulate wealth would depend upon one's own ability to protect one's possession of property using sufficient force to discourage the many interlopers who otherwise would take that wealth as their own by stealth or by force. In a world without social organization, the alpha male would possess the wealth to the extent that there was any wealth to be possessed, but only so long as he were able to defend his stash from the aggressive behavior of others, the next alpha male on the horizon. Only humanity's propensities to organize into societies, and to create and maintain social and political institutions, permit the acquisition and preservation of wealth beyond one's natural short-lived ability to physically intimidate competitors who would take that wealth away.

What lessons about taxes are we to learn from this regarding our views of fairness and justice? They are and can only be that the benefits of the social compact (social, political, and economic organization), in economic terms, are enjoyed by individuals in society most nearly in direct proportion to their wealth. This is a fundamental tenet to understanding the moral imperative of the *Fair Tax System* as presented in this book.

The modest proposal of this book is that the burden of taxation should, then, be borne in direct proportion to one's wealth, and, with one exception, only one's wealth. While this idea may appear radical, it can only be said to be radical for three reasons. First, no one alive can remember when taxes were assessed based on wealth at all. Second, wealth in our society, in fact, remains almost untaxed. Third, if such a system were adopted, so much would change.

I try in this book to carefully analyze how such a system would work, how it might be implemented, and how things would change if taxes were based solely upon wealth.

CHAPTER 3

✧ ✧ ✧

A Brief History of Tax

An entire book could be devoted to the history of taxation alone. Since no such history is needed here to make the essential point, only a summary review is presented[1].

The oldest known tax system was imposed 6,000 years ago at a place called Lagash, one of the oldest cities of Sumer and of later Babylonia. Our information about this comes from clay tablets that were unearthed in an archeological dig. These first known taxes were instituted to finance a war. To collect them, tax collectors armed with the power of seizure stretched from one end of the land to the other. Afterward, the tax collectors refused to give up their power to tax. As a result, a saying arose that circulated in those ancient societies. "You can have a lord, you can have a king, but the man to fear is the tax collector." Not surprisingly Lagash became the site of history's first known tax rebellion.

The Pharaonic reigns of the great Egyptian civilization left prodigious records of tax collections. In Egypt, the Pharaoh's scribes,

---

[1] If the reader would like to read about the history of taxation in more detail, there are very few good books available and reasonably priced. Two worth considering are *Federal Taxation in America: A Short History* (Woodrow Wilson Center Press, paperback) by W. Elliott Brownlee and *A History of Taxation and Expenditure in the Western World* by Carolyn Webber and Aaron Wildavsky (Simon & Schuster, 1986), out of print but widely available in used bookstores and through Amazon.com.

managed and supervised by the Pharaoh's Vizier, were the tax collectors. The Vizier was head of the Pharaoh's government and served as prime minister, chief justice, and head of the treasury. He was the court of last resort only beneath the Pharaoh himself. Vizier was the position that Joseph came to occupy in the Old Testament story, later to become retold in an Andrew Lloyd Webber musical, first in London's West End and then on Broadway, entitled *Joseph and the Amazing Technicolor Dreamcoat*. Ancient documents reveal that during one period, the Vizier went so far as to impose a tax on cooking oil that was left to the scribes to collect. To ensure that citizens were not avoiding the cooking oil tax, scribes would enter households and audit the goods contained in the household.

The revenue of Athens in the fifth century BC, the historical apex of the development of Athenian civilization and influence, was mainly derived from tribute paid by her subjects. Athenian citizens paid no tax. No more than 20% of its population were citizens. The elite in Athens taxed the common man. It was only in time of war that a direct tax was levied upon the citizens. This elitist distribution of power afforded its citizens the leisure required by them for the famous Athenian experiment in direct democracy, as opposed to the representational democracies of today. It lasted until 322 BC.

Athenians imposed a monthly tax on any resident who did not have both an Athenian mother and father. The tax was one drachma for men and a half drachma for women. This tax was referred to as Metoikion.

By the age of Demosthenes, about 350 BC, revenue derived from the Athenian Confederacy had become insignificant as noncitizens had little to offer in currency. The whole burden of the expenses of war, then, fell upon the 1200 richest citizens, who were made subject to direct taxation in the dual forms of the Trierachy and the Eisphora. The former was a system whereby individual citizens furnished and maintained triremes (the fleet warships of the era, manned by scores of oarsmen) as a part of their public duty. The latter was a form of direct tax on wealth imposed upon the value of the property or the estate of the citizen and paid in currency.

The Greeks, it turns out, were one of the few societies that succeeded in rescinding a tax once the emergency that gave rise to its necessity was over. Once additional resources in the form of booty were obtained in the war effort, these resources were used to refund the tax to those citizens who paid it. Hence, the beginning of borrowing to meet government shortfall was invented on a *de facto* basis.

History shows that those who are in power finance the advantages they enjoy on the backs of those without power. Athens of the fifth century is but one of many examples.

The earliest taxes in Rome, called Portoria, were customs duties imposed on imports and exports. During the time of Julius Caesar, who was elected consul in 59 BC, a 1% sales tax was imposed.

Caesar Augustus raised the sales tax to 4% on slaves, retaining a 1% tax on everything else. He reigned from 27 BC to 14 AD. He contributed to tax history by instituting the first inheritance tax imposed to provide retirement funds for the military. The tax was 5% on all inheritances except lifetime gifts to children and spouses. The English and Dutch referred to the inheritance tax of Augustus in developing their own inheritance tax systems.

In 60 AD, Boadicea, queen of East Anglia, led a revolt that can be attributed to corrupt Roman tax collectors in the British Isles. Allegedly all Roman soldiers within 100 miles were killed and London was seized. Some estimate that over 80,000 people were killed during the revolt. Ultimately, the revolt was crushed by the Roman Emperor Nero, and new administrators were appointed for the British Isles.

In English history from 991 AD onward, taxes called Danegeld and Heregeld were imposed by Anglo-Saxon kings on land and private personal property. These taxes were first imposed to afford the payment of tribute to the Vikings. After the Norman Conquest in 1066, Denegeld was revived and was levied until 1162 to finance military operations.

Denegeld, interestingly, provides the back story for the famous ride of Lady Godiva. According to legend, Lady Godiva's husband, Leofric, Earl of Mercia, foreswore to reduce the high taxes he levied on the residents of his wife's beloved hometown of Coventry only when she would ride naked through the streets of the town. In other words, he assumed, never. But he underestimated his wife's love of Coventry and its inhabitants or overestimated her modesty.

According to one version of the legend, Lady Godiva's long hair covered her body during her ride so that her full nakedness was not revealed. According to another version, at Godiva's request, everyone stayed indoors on the day of her ride on market day, except for the infamous "Peeping Tom." Whichever version is true, her husband considered it a miracle that his beautiful wife's nakedness was not publicly observed. He was so grateful that he not only reduced the tax but funded the convent to be built in Coventry.

The Anglo-Saxon and Norman kings also imposed substantial customs duties.

The Hundred Years' War between England and France was fought between 1337 and 1453. One of the key factors that renewed fighting in 1369 was the rebellion of the nobles of Aquitaine over the oppressive tax policies of Edward, The Black Prince.

Taxes during the fourteenth century in England were very progressive. The 1377 Poll Tax imposed a tax on the Duke of Lancaster that was 520 times the tax on the common peasant. Under the earliest taxing schemes at that time, an income tax was imposed on the wealthy, office holders, and the clergy. A tax on movable property was imposed on merchants. The poor paid little or no taxes.

King Charles I had problems with Parliament that arose because of a disagreement in 1629 about the rights of taxation afforded the king and the rights of taxation afforded the Parliament. The king was ultimately charged with treason and beheaded, confirming beyond any doubt that the power of the Parliament was on the ascendency in England, and the power of the monarchy in decline.

In 1643, to pay for the army commanded by Oliver Cromwell, Parliament imposed excise taxes on essential commodities (grain, meat, etc.). An excise tax is a tax levied on the manufacture, sale, or consumption of a commodity. These taxes extracted even more funds than those imposed by Charles I, especially from the poor. The excise tax, ironically imposed through the legislative authority of Parliament, one of the first experiments in representational democracy, was very regressive, increasing the tax on the poor so much that the Smithfield riots occurred in 1647. The riots occurred because the new taxes lowered rural laborers' ability to buy wheat to the point where a family of four would starve.

Continuing with Parliament's flexing its power over those without power, colonists were required to pay taxes under the Molasses Act. The Molasses Act was modified by Parliament in 1764 to include import duties on foreign molasses, sugar, wine, and other commodities. The new act was known as the Sugar Act. Parliament added the Stamp Act in 1765. The Stamp Act imposed a direct tax on all newspapers printed in the British colonies and most commercial and legal documents. And, of course, everyone educated in American schools knows of the Boston Tea Party, a political demonstration in reaction to the effrontery of Parliament in its imposition of a tax on tea. "No taxation without representation" became the siren call of the American Revolution.

Soon after Americans ousted inequitable British taxation, Secretary of Finance Alexander Hamilton, in 1791, decided to implement his plan to put the new nation on steady financial footing by imposing the first American excise tax on whiskey makers. The tax, though, favored large distillers over small farmers with stills in the mountains of Pennsylvania, Maryland, and Virginia. The farmers, memories fresh from the revolution against British economic tyranny, incited their own new revolution—a challenge to the sovereignty of the new government and the power of the wealthy eastern seaboard establishment. In 1794, settlers west of the Alleghenies started what is now known as the "Whiskey Rebellion." They rioted against the tax collectors. President Washington eventually sent troops to quell the riots. Although two settlers were eventually convicted of treason, the president granted each a pardon.

In 1798 Congress enacted a federal direct tax on real property to pay for the expansion of the army and navy in preparation for an anticipated war with France. The tax was widely resented. An armed group of German immigrant farmers, led by John Fries, forced the release of tax resisters who were being held by federal marshals. The then president, John Adams, sent federal troops to arrest him and those that joined him in rebellion. Fries was convicted of treason, and though no one had been injured or killed in the insurrection, he was sentenced to be hanged. President Adams pardoned him in 1800. In one of the great ironies of American tax history, Fries had been the leader of a militia unit that had been sent out to suppress the "Whiskey Rebellion."

A precursor to the modern income tax that we know today was invented by the British in 1798 to finance their engagement in the war with Napoleon. The tax imposed by the British Tax Act of 1798 was repealed in 1816, and opponents of the tax, who thought it should only be used to finance wars, wanted all records of the tax destroyed along with its repeal. Records were publicly burned by the Chancellor of the Exchequer, but copies were retained in the basement of the tax court.

The first income tax suggested in the United States was during the War of 1812. The tax, based on the British Tax Act of 1798, was never imposed because the treaty of Ghent was signed in 1815 and ended hostilities. The need for the additional revenue was therefore eliminated for a time.

America's Tax Act of 1861 proposed a tax to "be levied, collected, and paid, upon annual income of every person residing in the U.S. whether derived from any kind of property, or from any professional trade, employment, or vocation carried on in the United States or elsewhere, or from any source whatever." It was passed but never put in force. Rates under the act were 3% on income above $800 per year and 5% on the income of Americans living outside the US.

The Tax Act of 1862 was passed and signed by President Lincoln on July 1, 1862. The rates were 3% on income above $600 per year and 5% on income above $10,000. The rent paid or the rental value of one's home could be deducted from income in determining the tax liability.

The Tax Act of 1864 was passed to raise additional revenue to support the Civil War. Senator Garret Davis stated in the Congressional Record that the act was consistent with the "recognition of the idea that taxes shall be paid according to the abilities of a person to pay." The rhetoric held up a commendable ideal that, like today, was not met. Tax rates were 5% for annual income between $600 and $5000, 7.5% for income between $5001 and $10,000 and 10% on income above $10,000. The deduction for rent or rental value was limited to $200. Further deduction for the cost of repairs was allowed.

The Commissioner of Revenue stated, "The people of this country have accepted it with cheerfulness, to meet a temporary exigency, and it has excited no serious complaint in its administration." Any acceptance, in fact, was primarily due to the need for revenue to finance the Civil War. Although the people may have "cheerfully accepted the tax," compliance was not high. Figures released after the Civil War indicated that 276,661 people filed tax returns in 1870 (the year of the highest number of returns filed). The country's population was then approximately 38 million.

With the end of the Civil War, the public's "accepted cheerfulness" regarding taxation waned. The Tax Act of 1864 was modified after the war. The rates were changed to a flat 5% with the exemption amount raised to $1,000. By 1869, there had been attempts to make the tax permanent, but in the words of the *New York Times*, "No businessman could pass the day without suffering from those burdens." From 1870 to 1872, the rate was a flat 2.5%, and the exemption amount was raised to $2,000.

The tax was repealed in 1872. In its place were installed significant tariffs that served as the major revenue source for the United States until 1913. In 1913, the 16th Amendment was passed, which allowed Congress authority to tax the citizenry on income from whatever source derived.

Of course, all during these times, the States had retained the authority to tax and generally relied upon taxes on real estate, personal property, and sales taxes.

During the 1930s, federal individual income taxes never totaled more than 1.4% of the Gross National Product (GNP). Corporate income taxes never more than 1.6% of GNP. In 1990, those same taxes as a percentage of GNP were 8.77 and 1.99 respectively. One can see that corporations have fared much better than people in this regard, even though the growth of corporate wealth and income during this period is staggering.

Of course, my selection of the specifics in this historical survey is somewhat arbitrary and, I admit, slanted to an American audience. But the pattern of taxation seen here is generally paralleled in virtually every society in Western civilization.

Suffice it to say, initially the wealthy were taxed for the same reason that Bonnie and Clyde robbed banks. That's where the money (wealth) was to be found. While the wealthy are still taxed to some extent, government, more and more, has found it convenient to tax income and to tax certain transactions, from sales to car registrations, a predilection that relative to net worth strongly favors the wealthy.

Why is the history of taxation as it is? The question is rhetorical as the answer should be obvious. Regressive taxation is fundamentally beneficial to the wealthy and powerful. Tax policy as it now exists is, in fact, tax welfare for the rich.

While this statement may seem confrontational, it is not meant to be. Economic class warfare is not the point. Economic class warfare has already existed below the radar screen of the body politic for a long, long time and still does. The wealthy have been winning a war of distraction. The middle class and the poor have been losing badly. Rather, the statement is meant to be provocative. It is meant to provoke some deep thought about how and why we tax. Hopefully an informed electorate, at least in Western democracies, can change toward the Fair Tax System. The Fair Tax System is a moral imperative for our age. Morally it is as necessary as finding a fix for problems of global warming, pollution, and the depletion of our oceans' ecosystems.

CHAPTER 4

✧ ✧ ✧

What Fair Looks Like

Before considering any of the ramifications of a fair tax system, let's consider what a fair tax system is. What would it look like?

Per Capita Taxation

Everyone in the "village" counts. Everyone should be counted a member of society. A fair tax system, therefore, would have some small annual tax paid by or on behalf of everyone in society.

Equitable Allocation of Tax Burden

Beyond such a per capita tax, a fair tax system would equitably allocate the economic cost of government in all its various forms and programs. "Equitably" means in proportion to the benefit, in monetary terms, that an organized society accords to each taxpayer. Each person should pay for the relative benefits that each person receives.

Periodic Redistribution of Wealth

Finally, a fair tax system would avoid the concentration of wealth in too few hands for too long. Read these last three points again. It's worth it. Don't they make sense?

*****

At this point you might be asking, "Where does he get that from?" Especially that last one? "What moral authority is there for this particular judgment of what is 'fair'?" Well, fair enough.

Moral Authority from Religious Traditions

If authority is needed beyond "common sense" (a most uncommon commodity), one can find support for this formula in the sacred texts of various religions.

The book of Exodus is the second book of the Pentateuch (also known as The Five Books of Moses or the Torah). Arguably, the Pentateuch is the text which informs the foundational ethics of all Western civilization. The case is made powerfully in Thomas Cahill's bestseller, *The Gifts of the Jews: How a Tribe of Desert Nomads Changed the Way Everyone Thinks and Feels* (Doubleday 1999).

The book of Exodus, chapter 30, verses 11–17 most directly support the first idea, a small tax applied to and for every person in the country.

The text requires the giving of a half-*shekel* by sanctuary weight for each person to be counted among the people of Israel. In giving the half-*shekel*, the Torah explicitly commands that "the rich shall not give more, and the poor shall not give less." By contributing only this small sum—and *no more*—each Jew became a full partner in the society and its destiny. Literally pages and pages of biblical commentary over 1,800 years or more testify to the understanding that in this way, God assures his people that every member of society is counted and counts.

The second idea of what constitutes a fair tax system is supported by many references.

In Deuteronomy, the last of the Five Books of Moses, chapter 26, verse 12, the people are commanded to tithe every third year. We are all familiar with the expression to tithe, but in the biblical sense, tithing was not limited to the tithing of income, but rather it required the tithing of the wealth that God bestowed upon those people. The tithe of this verse is required to be made to the benefit of (a) the community, (b) the Levites who have no portion, and (c) the widow and orphan. Thus, an obligation is imposed upon those blessed with wealth to dedicate a portion of their wealth, here 10% every three years, to the benefit of those without wealth. This formula, slightly more than 3% per year when understood as compound interest, was a perfect prescription for a tax proportional to one's wealth or material blessings.

Leviticus, too, the fourth book, is explicit in its requirement that sacrifices in the temple are to be offered according to the means of the person offering sacrifice. So too, in various biblical citations, is the command to leave the corners of the field for the poor. Tzedakah is typically translated in English as charity, or the idea of benefiting others less fortunate. But in the Old Testament, it is not an option as the English translation might imply, but rather an obligation.

Nor is the concept foreign to the Christian Bible. In Luke 12:48, it states, "For unto whomsoever much is given, of him shall be much required: and to whom men have committed much, of him they will ask the more."

Chapter 18, verse 17, of the Book of Mosiah, one of the books that make up the Book of Mormon states, "[T]he people…should impart of their substance, everyone according to that which he has. If he has more abundantly, he should impart more abundantly; and of him that has but little, but little should be required. And to him that had not should be given."

I am sure that everyone who has studied any religious tradition can point to religious principles articulated within that tradition that similarly require of society what one might call economic justice.

But where is the authority for the last principle, preventing the concentration of wealth in the hands of a few from generation to generation?

Again, here we look first to Deuteronomy. It requires creditors to forgive the debts of other Israelites every seven years and warns against allowing this law of debt forgiveness to become a factor in giving or denying loans to the needy in the first place. Thus, Deuteronomy tells us, "There shall be no poverty or want in the land." This requirement lends support to the biblical notion of fairness, a notion that periodically requires the redistribution of wealth. A similar requirement exists in the Qur'an, the "bible" of Islam.

Back to the Old Testament, God's justification for the redemption of the Jews in the time of Moses from their subjugation in Egypt is the creation of a society that will serve as "a light unto the nations." Likewise, this is the explicit justification for God's covenant with His chosen people at Mt. Sinai. In such a society, as prescribed in Exodus and Numbers, two of the Five Books of Moses, God requires that the land promised to the patriarch, Abraham, the "Promised Land," be distributed initially in equal parts to the twelve tribes of Israel according to their number. In this way, everyone begins their new life with an equal chance for prosperity and sustenance.

Then in Leviticus, we find the command to redistribute land back to the original tribes every fifty years, in the Jubilee Year. This redistribution of land every generation, the forgiveness of debt, and the freeing of those indentured into servitude are all biblical requirements of the Jubilee year (fiftieth year). These laws affirm the biblical understanding that the source of all wealth is the Creator, and if wealth belongs to anyone, it belongs to all humanity. It does not belong to any one person, family, generation, or tribe.

This is not to say that private property has no place in the Old Testament. Private property rights in chattel are implicitly recognized in many references, as are rights in land, but not rights to own land or other property in perpetuity.

In a just society, therefore, according to the world's great religions, fairness and economic justice require a periodic redistribution of wealth and property. Why? Because a periodic redistribution of life's material resources will assure to each generation a fair and equitable chance to pursue happiness in life. It provides a more level playing field, if you will. It also reminds those that do enjoy abundance during their lifetimes that their good fortunes were not secured by their own virtue alone. But rather it is by the virtue of a system maintained and supported by society and, in religious terms, by the grace and generosity of divine power.

Like the history of taxation, an entire book could be presented ferreting out of religious traditions' support for the idea that a fair tax system should include certain characteristics. I don't pretend to be a religious scholar. So I will leave that task to those who care to pursue the study in greater depth. Suffice it to say that the scriptures cited reflect a few of those portions of "divine revelation" that underlie my thinking about the proposed Fair Tax System's three requirements based in morality and ethics.

One need not look to religious inspiration, though, to see the fairness and justice behind the proposed Fair Tax System. You will see, as we continue our exposition of the Fair Tax System, that the three legs upon which the Fair Tax System stand are also well justified by political, social, and economic theory and by the practical realities of our lives.

Now, What Might Such a System Look Like?

The first requirement is easy to accomplish. Each family would pay a nominal amount for each person alive. In today's terms, this might be something like $100 or $200 per person annually. Parents would pay the annual tax for themselves and each of their minor children. With 300,000,000 people in the United States today, $150 per person would provide $45 billion in tax revenue. If it were $200, then $60 billion. In this way, everyone is counted, and everyone counts. Everyone has paid for his or her stake in society.

Of course, in modern society, there are many more legal persons, e.g. corporations, limited liability companies, limited partnerships, etc. These entities are legal fictions or creations. Under the law, they enjoy certain advantages of their distinct legal personhoods, advantages that extend to the benefit of the owners, officers, directors, and employees of these entities, but mostly to the owners, officers, and directors. As a creation of law, they too, in fairness, should be counted.

I will endeavor to give an estimate of the revenue available from this source even though not based upon definitive data. My figures are taken from various sources, many available on the internet. As you will come to appreciate, the accuracy of these calculations is irrelevant to the premise of the Fair Tax System. But calculations even based upon rough data are helpful to quantify the additional revenue available from these entities.

There are approximately 13,000 publicly traded companies in the United States. This does not include wholly owned subsidiaries, though wholly owned subsidiaries should count. There are about 3.3 million S-corporations operating in the United States. S-corporations are closely held (nonpublic) corporations that for most purposes elect to be taxed as a partnership. There are also 3,600 or so closely held C-corporations which are nonpublic corporations that choose to be taxed as a corporation. About 1.7 million business enterprises are organized as limited liability companies other than corporations. There are about 1,550 partnerships. This totals 5,005,150 business enterprises that enjoy some legal status separate and distinct from the beneficial owners. At $150 per enterprise, over three quarters of a billion in revenue would be raised in taxes; at $200, over a billion.

Interestingly, in most states, business enterprises pay considerably more than $200 per year simply by virtue of their legal existence. In California, for instance, each corporation or limited liability company pays a minimum state franchise tax of $800 per year. In the Fair Tax System, these other fees (taxes) would be eliminated.

Then there are approximately 1.2 million nonprofit organizations in the United States, many that qualify as charities and some that don't. They would collectively pay per capita tax revenue of $180–$240 million annually, at respectively $150 and $200 per entity, simply because they exist.

As can be seen in Table 1 below, in total, this flat per capita tax of $150–$200 per natural or legal person would provide annual revenue for the administration of government services of about $46–$61.2 billion.

Table 1: Tax revenue based upon $150 and $200 per legal person

Per Capita Tax Revenue Category of Taxpayer	Number	At $150	At $200
People	300,000,000	$45,000,000,000	$60,000,000,000
Publicly Traded Corps	13,000	$1,950,000	$2,600,000
S-Corporations	3,300,000	$495,000,000	$660,000,000
C-Corporations	3,600	$540,000	$720,000
LLCs	1,700,000	$255,000,000	340,000,000
Partnerships	1,550	$232,500	$310,000
Nonprofits	1,200,000	$180,000,000	$240,000,000
Total		$45,932,722,500	$61,243,630,000

These sums fall far short of the amount needed to pay for government services in the United States, but this revenue is certainly significant. In words often but perhaps erroneously ascribed to the late senator Everett McKinley Dirksen, "A billion here, a billion there, and pretty soon you're talking real money."

Fair Tax on Wealth

Still, there would be two other revenue sources in a fair tax system. One would be paid annually in proportion to the economic benefit received by the taxpayer from the social and political order. It would therefore be based upon an annual assessment of the taxpayer's net wealth. Exactly how this could be assessed and reported are details which are discussed in a later chapter. But it is useful here to get an idea of what percentage of wealth would be needed to finance current levels of government spending.

How Much $$$ Is Needed to Pay for the Current Level of Government

I reference levels of government spending rather than levels of taxation because taxes are only one source of funds used by our governments. Other sources of funds that governments use are (1) the sale or lease of assets owned by the government and (2) borrowing through selling government bonds (long term) or notes (short term.) The latter source, borrowing, is particularly offensive to the Fair Tax System. Why? Because the money that the government borrows comes from the wealthy in this country and abroad. Borrowing from the wealthy in this country is much like having them pay taxes and then giving them a promissory note or IOU signed by the government to repay those tax dollars, with interest on behalf of its citizens, present and future. Borrowing from foreign nationals, and worse, from foreign governments raises deep concerns about the consequences of hocking the country's assets and future to foreign nationals or foreign powers.

As to borrowing from foreign persons or entities, it is sometimes argued that these loans give them a stake in the success of our society and its economy. This advantage though is better served by allowing foreign investment in our assets, our businesses, our technology, etc. No greater stake is created by loans made by them directly to the government. If anything, such loans put foreign interests in the position of exercising undue influence over our political decision-making apparatus.

Then too, borrowing raises the moral issue of mortgaging the future, our children's future, for the expenditures we want to make today. It is the moral equivalent of parents who would borrow money and create debt for their children and grandchildren to repay.

Under a fair tax system, there would be no borrowing, except perhaps to pay for capital expenditures for infrastructure investments that have a predictable useful life. The benefit of such projects could then be amortized over their useful lives and be paid for as the benefits were being enjoyed by those enjoying the benefits.

If the government is largely out of the borrowing business, the demand for debt financing will decline relative to the supply of funds available for loans, reducing interest rates across the board. Interest rates, of course, reflect the cost of borrowing money and, like all prices, are responsive to supply and demand. It was President Clinton who so cogently made and proved the point that high interest rates are a hidden tax, the burden of which is borne disproportionately by the poor, the middle class, and the young. But unlike taxes collected by the treasury and used to pay the cost of governments programs that society deems worthy, interest rates on loans to government and higher interest rates on loans generally go directly to the wealthiest in our society.

How much, then, does it cost to run our society here in America?

According to the US Census Bureau's Consolidated Federal Funds Report for Fiscal Year 2004, total federal expenditures were a little more than $2,262 billion or $2.262 trillion. According to US Census Bureau statistics, state and local governments combined spent roughly $2,435 billion or $2.435 trillion in fiscal year 2003–2004. The total then represents a fair estimate of the spending of all government in the United States and in its territories in one year, 2004. To keep it simple, I have rounded up to $4,700 billion or $4.7 trillion per year.

Once the body politic decides, as it evidently has, to spend for government and the services, infrastructure and public assets government supports, the next question, and a separate question, is how to fairly pay the bill.

Since we are proposing an annual flat tax on wealth, we need to know the total net worth of those who would pay taxes to support these expenditures.

There are no reliable figures on this from any one source. I will try to provide a good approximation from multiple sources. Again, exactitude is not necessary to make the point. Rough calculations will serve adequately.

According to a 2002 Report in the *Executive Intelligence Weekly*, the total value of single-family residences in America alone was over $12 trillion. Even with the devaluation of housing in 2007 and 2008, it is a good bet that values still meet or exceed those levels in 2002. Any knowledge about what has happened to the housing market since then will convince the reader that this is still a conservative estimate of value. This does not represent rental properties, offices, warehouses, retail stores, farms, recreation properties, amusement parks, churches and synagogues, etc.

In 1996, 51 million individuals and 10,000 institutional investors owned stocks or shares in mutual funds traded on the NYSE. In December 1997, the total value of all publicly traded stocks traded on the New York Stock Exchange alone was reported to be $9.413 trillion. By 2005, according to the 2005 report of Equity Ownership in America by the Investment Company Institute and the Securities Industry Association, 56 million households in the US owned publicly traded equities either directly or in mutual fund shares, worth approximately $12.376 trillion. These do not include the value of the shares of the individual securities owned by the mutual funds.

The two other major stock markets in the United States are the American Stock Exchange (AMEX) and the NASDAQ (National Association of Securities Dealers).

The total value of debt instruments publicly traded on the exchanges in a year in the US alone has been estimated at $90–$100 trillion, with US government securities constituting the overwhelming part of the total. Of course, with implementation of the Fair Tax System as proposed, the government securities would be largely paid off with tax revenues and disappear. But the funds now loaned to government would largely find their way into other competing investment instruments or assets.

An estimated 11,000 other equity securities are traded over the counter, issues that generally are too small to qualify for inclusion in the computerized NASDAQ market or for listing on an exchange. These issues continue to be traded with the aid of the "pink sheets," daily bulletins that indicate which firms make markets in these stocks, but seldom quote bid and asked prices. The aggregate share and dollar volume in these securities is significant but very small, as compared to the NASDAQ, and not accounted for in this analysis.

The International Monetary Fund reports that in 2001, M1 (an aggregate of currency and demand deposits) was equal to $1,595.5 billion or $1.5955 trillion. In that same year, M2 (an aggregate equal to M1 plus savings deposits, small time-deposits, and money market mutual funds) was $6.9612 trillion.

All the companies that publicly sell their shares own assets as well. The net value of those assets can generally be understood to be the total of the value of all equity shares in the companies. The assets, of course, include good will and other intangible assets of the business, which are valued through the public's trading of stock on the stock exchanges.

Extrapolating from all these figures suggests a conservative estimate of net worth from investment securities and the assets owned by companies that issue securities to be about $250 trillion.

Although no authoritative number has been found at this juncture, $100 trillion seems a conservative estimate of the value of all nonsingle family home real estate in the United States and its territories. Of course, a lot of this would be assets owned by corporations, churches, charities, foundations, universities, or other business entities that issue securities. For that reason, so as not to double count, I am using $60 trillion in my estimates. Small businesses and other non-real estate family assets represent the bulk of the remaining assets in the US.

According to *Entrepreneur* magazine, in 2003 the estimated total number of small businesses in the United States was 22,659,000, producing $858.9 billion in income for the proprietors. This means that after expenses, $858.9 billion is the gross profit generated to the proprietors. Assuming an average enterprise value of only three times the gross profit for small businesses, these businesses should be worth about $2.5 trillion.

Gross private savings totaled about 1.3 trillion in 1999 according to the US Bureau of Economic Analysis.

How many additional trillions are in the hands of churches, mosques, synagogues, university endowments, and other nonprofit charitable organizations? These too benefit from the organization of society into its political and social institutions and are dependent upon it for their acquisition and retention of wealth. A fair tax system would require an equal contribution by these organizations based upon wealth. For the purpose of this analysis, we will assume $3 trillion here.

Doing the math, without any further consideration of value of other assets that may not be accounted for by these rough numbers (such as commodities contracts, commodities options, insurance cash value, mutual insurance companies, etc.), the wealth of this country and its citizens totals conservatively approximately $400 trillion even though I have counted only $350 trillion.

Table 2: Rough calculation of total value of all taxable wealth, measured in thousands

Total Value of All Wealth Category	(Thousands) Value
Single Family Homes	$12,000,000,000
Household Owned Securities	$12,376,000,000
M2	$6,961,200,000
Est. Net Worth of Companies	$250,000,000,000
Nonsingle Family Home RE	$60,000,000,000
Small Businesses	$2,500,000,000
Nonprofit Charities	$3,000,000,000
Total	$346,837,200,000

About $4.7 trillion, you will recall, is the total of expenditures in the US for all federal, state, and local governments. This is only about 1.56% of the total wealth. To be certain that my rough calculations are conservative, I have rounded down the total of all assets and rounded up the percentage of wealth needed to pay the bills to 2%. Therefore, "the 2% solution."

If every "person" in the United States were taxed and paid annually only 2% of their net worth, there would be more than enough revenue to pay every bill of every level of government without imposing any sales tax, use tax, income tax, duties, real property tax, *ad valorem* (added value) taxes, excise taxes, car registration fees, driver's license fees, tolls, public facility admission fees, park fees, etc. And all this would be paid without borrowing.

Some Examples of How Such a Wealth Tax Would Allocate Tax Burden

The total tax liability of a family of four with a zero or negative net worth would be $800 per year at a $200 flat tax per person. The same family with a net worth of $100,000 would be $2,800 per year. The total tax liability for a family of four worth $1.5 million would be $30,800. The total annual tax of billionaire Bob worth one billion, with his family of four, would be $20,000,800.

Table 3: Comparison of tax liability under fair tax system (per capita tax and 2% of net worth) for family of four with zero or negative net worth, family of four with $100,000 of net worth, family of four with $1,500,000 of net worth, and for family of four with $1 billion of net worth, at $150 per capita tax and at $200 per capita tax

Tax Liability Comparison		
Family of 4	At $150 per capita	At $200 per capita
w/ 0 or Neg. Net Worth	$600	$800
w/ $100,000. Net Worth	$2,600	$2,800
w/ $1.5MM Net Worth	$30,600	$30,800
w/ $1,000 MM Net Worth	$20,000,600	$20,000,800

Intergenerational Transfer Tax

Of course, 2% (or less) would be the percentage if we needed to finance all government spending through these two taxes alone. This is considerably less that the roughly 3% called for in Deuteronomy. The final element of a fair tax system is to tax the intergenerational transfer of wealth.

Here, a balance needs to be struck between competing values.

One motive for the accumulation of wealth is at least partly to be able to pass wealth on to one's children. But there should, in fairness to society, be a limit to the extent that we protect this interest.

Children of the wealthy already enjoy great benefits from their parents' wealth during the parents' lifetime. They enjoy the benefits of superior educational and cultural advantages. Parental and other peer modeling results in different expectations of and desires for a certain quality of life. Children of the wealthy go to the best schools; they are encouraged to live up to different expectations, enjoy the benefit of friendships and relationships with other families of wealth and power, obtain opportunities to work, and invest not typically available to others. These are just a few of the many advantages they enjoy over other children.

Certainly, though, a case can be made for allowing a family to accumulate some wealth to pass along to their own children without tax. But how much is enough? How much is justified? One million? Ten million? How much?

Whatever the amount, fairness would again demand that the bulk of the value of one's estate beyond that amount should be taxed heavily. In other words, if we decide as a society that every set of parents should be able to freely pass on to their children or loved ones, say, $5,000,000, we could allow assets equal in value to $5,000,000 to be given without any gift or inheritance tax, and tax amounts over $5,000,000 at, say 75%, or 80%. This is not too onerous, even to the very wealthy.

First, let's acknowledge that the tax would affect very few families since only a small percentage enjoys a net worth of over $5MM (perhaps .25%). The estate tax as of 2011 was charged on amounts over $1,000,000 and affected only a small percentage of people (about 1%). That is why it is rhetorical overkill to call the tax a death tax. We do not tax death at all. It is a tax on the passing of estates, not on dying. And only those with sizable estates, a very small percentage of the population, pay any tax at all.

If Mr. and Mrs. Megabucks have, say, $120 MM in assets, under the Fair Tax System, they could, years before their deaths, still transfer $5MM to their children. If they gave $5MM in the form of appreciating assets, then when the parents die, the $5MM in assets they transferred, say fifteen or twenty years earlier, might be worth $20MM or more. And so, as measured at the time of their deaths, they gave not $5 MM to their children without tax but $20 MM. If the Megabucks have $120MM remaining when they die and the tax on estates over $5MM were 75%, $30MM of those funds would go to their children and $90MM to the government in taxes. Those poor children of Mr. and Mrs. Megabucks would only inherit $50MM from their parents, measured at the time of their deaths.

The gift and inheritance taxes collected could, of course, go into the general fund and pay for ongoing government programs. If this were the political choice, it could enable a reduction in the tax rate charged on net worth in the annual wealth tax. Or these taxes could be used to supplement and support additional social and government programs designed to level the playing field for everyone else in society, programs that benefit children of the middle class and the poor, such as increased access to childcare, Head Start, parent training, scholarships for university education, small business administration loan programs, microlending programs, poverty housing programs, etc.

In this way, many of our human resources, the lives of disadvantaged children, can be salvaged and supported, maximizing, to the extent possible, the benefits that they will give to and minimizing the detriment they otherwise would inflict upon society. A golden age could be ushered in as the personal talents of more people in society are nurtured and supported as their demonstrated talents merit, yielding great returns to us all. Programs such as universal health care, improved education at all levels, job training and retraining, support for scientific research in areas needed by society but for which the financial returns are too uncertain to be justified by private enterprise alone are all worthy candidates.

This would likely produce ripple effects as well in areas such as the reduction of crime and improvement of health, saving billions already represented as costs paid in current government expenditures. These savings too can then be redirected or used to either reduce the annual tax rates on wealth, or better yet, to be reinvested in our society as is determined by the political system considering the common weal.

Making Possible the Public Financing of Elections

One terribly important area in which these extra tax dollars can be directed is to the public financing of elections.

Most people today agree that our government needs to be more responsive to the needs of its citizens, and that if elections were publicly financed and political contributions to campaigns prohibited or severely limited, we would enjoy better government that is not perverted by the influence of special interests. In the words of Thom Hartmann, author of *Screwed: The Undeclared War against the Middle Class—and What We Can Do about It*, public financing of elections would return the government to "we the people."

But there is no appetite to insist upon this as a litmus test of support for candidates running for high office. Why? I suggest the answer is that whenever the proposal for public financing of campaigns is made, the question is raised, "How will we pay for it?" Then those with money, power, access, and influence, who oppose such a change so as to protect their ability to wield disproportionate power and influence, start the drumbeat that pulses through the mainstream information media jungle, drumbeats that warn, "If you support this change, you will be voting to raise your taxes."

I've found that when people oppose higher taxes to support new government programs, generally their opposition is based primarily upon their conscious or unconscious fear that their own tax liability will increase. The poor and middle class, who make up most voters, are overburdened already with taxes. So their fear is completely understandable. The Fair Tax System, uniquely, can become a reality first, because when the middle class or poor voter understands it, the overwhelming majority of our citizens will be willing to actively support it because they will see that it is in their own economic self-interest.

Once the Fair Tax System is implemented, our citizenry will no longer fear lending enthusiastic support for the public financing of election campaigns because the cost can be fully funded through the 2% solution, which will already have drastically reduced their tax burden and given them new hope for a brighter economic future. When public financing of election campaigns replaces our current system, lobbyists will be left to the only legitimate function they have, educating the legislature and the public in their areas of expertise and thereby assisting legislative bodies in rational decision-making for the benefit of the body politic, not the wealthy and powerful special interests.

Also, once the Fair Tax System replaces the existing patchwork quilt of federal, state, and local taxes and government-imposed fees for services, the wealthy and powerful will themselves have more incentive to encourage decision-making for the good of the body politic since they will be forced to pay their fair share of the cost of bad policy. Right now, as observed many times by Thom Hartmann on his radio broadcast on Air America, the policy supported by big corporations is to privatize profit and move expenses to the public sector. Since under the Fair Tax System big corporations will be paying taxes to finance government expenditures in proportion to their wealth, the incentive to maximize profit at the expense of "the commons" will substantially diminish.

That is why enacting the Fair Tax System is the single most important political change we can make. Only a fundamental redistribution of the tax burden to the wealthy, such as called for in the 2% solution, will allow for enough support to be galvanized to lead to the adoption of the public financing of campaigns.

Again, only the wealthiest among us will be required to increase what they already pay in taxes under the Fair Tax System. For most people, something like 99%, the Fair Tax System will substantially lower their tax burden. Voting their economic self-interest will save them money and add to the quality of their lives. What other cause could work so well as a rallying cry to the vast middle class? What other change in the way we do government can be successfully promoted as a litmus test to be applied for the support and the vote of the great majority of voting Americans than this? So "join and support the 2% Solution Revolution!"

CHAPTER 5

✧ ✧ ✧

Survey of Overall Benefits

Before getting into deeper detail, let's survey some of the overall benefits of the Fair Tax System.

Fairness

First, of course, is fairness.

Everybody pays something. Everybody thus demonstrates that they have a stake in the social order and counts as an equal member of society.

Then, as discussed earlier, under the Fair Tax System, those who benefit most in economic terms from the creation and maintenance of our society, its institutions, infrastructure, and laws pay during their lifetimes the costs of that social organization fairly, in direct proportion to the economic benefits they enjoy.

Finally, wealth beyond a politically determined level of legitimacy applicable to all is given back to society to use for its politically and democratically determined priorities, so that this wealth can be used to level the economic playing field for every member of society, irrespective of accidents of birth.

We have now a reality in which most of the cost of society is paid by a middle class forever squeezed in the system, a middle class dreaming, if not struggling, to become part of the economic elite that enjoys the overwhelming benefits and advantages of the system. This, we will see, is a natural consequence of a system of taxation based largely upon taxing income, consumption (sales taxes), and real estate based upon its gross value and not the taxpayer's equity. Why is that so? Let's examine each.

Income tax

Let's look at a common scenario, that of a renter with $45,000 of net assets who earns $60,000 per year of as compared to a professional with a net worth of $2,000,000 and $150,000 per year of earned income. That is the example of set forth in the table below:

Table 4: Illustration of tax inequity under current income tax system

Income		Net Worth	Income Tax	% of Net Worth
Mr. Professional	$150,000	$2,000,000	$45,000.00	2%
Joe Average	$ 60,000	$45,000	$ 18,000.00	40%

In each case I have assumed taxes of 30% only for the purpose of illustrating the principle. In reality, Mr. Professional will probably be paying significant mortgage interest reducing his taxable income. Further, social security taxes for Mr. Professional will stop once his income reaches the threshold of $97,500 for the 2007 taxable year. This means the 6.2% social security tax will be assessed on only that amount, and $52,500 of Mr. Professional's income will be free of social security tax. The effective social security tax rate as applied against his total earned income is 4.03%, about 2/3 of the tax rate assessed against Joe Average's income.

You can see, even in this simplified example, 30% of one's income is a much greater portion of a person's wealth when applied to some renter with $45,000 of net assets than it is for someone with $2,000,000 of net worth. Even though we apply the same rate to income in both cases, Joe is paying in income tax 40% of his net worth, while Megabucks is paying in income tax only 2% of his net worth.

Sales or use tax

While people of substantial net worth spend, in absolute terms, more money on taxable purchases than do poor and middle-class people, they spend far less relative to their wealth. Sales taxes, then, are inherently regressive. Look at the following example.

Table 5: Illustration of inequity of sales tax when viewed from the perspective of net worth

Taxed Spending		Net Worth	5% Sales Tax	% of Net Worth
Mr. Professional	$12,000	$2,000,000	$600	0.0300%
Joe Average	$5,000	$45,000	$250	0.5556%

In our example, Joe Average has been taxed about 1/2 of 1% (.55%) of his net worth from sales taxes, collected at 5% of taxable spending. Mr. Professional's spending is more than double that of Joe Average. Yet he has paid sales taxes of only 3/100 of 1% (.03%) of his net worth. That means that relative to his wealth, Joe Average has paid nearly twenty times more in sales tax than Mr. Professional.

It's true that the examples selected are somewhat arbitrary and do not necessarily represent any one or more real individuals. But even if we triple Megabucks' annual taxable spending to $36,000, the tax he pays is less than 1/10 of 1% (.09%) of his net worth. While the reality, person to person, may differ in specifics, the illustrated trend represents the essential reality.

The regressive nature of sales tax is by now so well-known to economists that I can make the assertion without citation. But in all the analyses of which I am aware, and there are many, the regressive nature of sales and use taxes is looked at from the perspective of income. When viewed from the perspective of net worth, it is more spectacularly so.

Real estate taxes

Right now, we assess and tax real estate on the basis of its gross value. If a wealthy man in California, in which real estate taxes equal roughly 1% of value, owns a $500,000 home free and clear, he is paying about $5,000 per year on taxes. That $5,000 then would represent 1% his net worth as represented by that house. If the same home is owned by a middle-class white-collar worker, with a $400,000 mortgage, he pays the same the $5,000 in property tax. The $5,000 tax he pays represents 5% of his net worth represented by that house.

In California, in response to rising property taxes, the state passed Proposition 13 by referendum. This "taxpayer revolution" did essentially two things. It prohibited property taxes from rising above 1% of property assessed value and prevented property from being reassessed unless and until sold to someone else. This bit of modern tax history exemplifies a couple of realities. The first is the political reality that when given the opportunity, voters will vote their pocketbooks. Remember this when we talk later about how to bring the Fair Tax System from concept to reality. The second reality is that Proposition 13, motivated by anger over unfairly rising taxes for all property owners, actually made the tax inequities in the system worse.

Now, as a result of Proposition 13, two identical houses can have wildly different assessed values depending upon when they were last sold. Ironically, the long-term property owner, who will likely possess a much larger equity than his neighbor, will pay far less in taxes. The newer owner, who will likely have far less equity than his neighbor, will pay much more in taxes. Look at the table below to see the point illustrated by an example.

Table 6: Illustration of inequity of property tax system

55-Year-Old Homeowner		35-Year-Old Homeowner	
Current Value	$360,000		$360,000
Mortgage	$0		$280,000
Equity	$360,000		$80,000
Year of Purchase	1970		2005
Purchase Price	$35,000		$350,000
Property Taxes	$350		$3,500
% of Equity	0.10%		4.38%

As you can see in the example above, the fifty-five-year-old homeowner has $360,000 in equity, which equals his wealth as represented by that house. His annual property taxes are 1/10 of 1% of his equity. The thirty-five-year-old homeowner is paying 4.38% of his equity (wealth) in property taxes. Yet society and the law equally protect the rights of each in their houses and the wealth that the houses represent to each. Could anything be more unfair?

As you can see, our current system increases the benefits of wealth for the wealthy and slants the economic and social playing field even more heavily in their favor.

Remove Tax Considerations from Economic Decision-Making

Another benefit of the Fair Tax System is that it would eliminate the skewing of economic decisions regarding investment and spending by tax policy. Many people don't realize the extent to which taxes affect decisions that result in the allocation capital resources in our economy.

One simple example, and probably the most common, can be found in the different tax treatment of earned income, dividend or interest income, and capital gains. Income is taxed as it is earned and received. Not much can be done to avoid or delay taxation when income is the result of one's labor or of the payment of interest and dividends. But income is a term of art, meaning that in tax terms, it is defined by tax law.

To fully understand the discussion, I want you to consider income as an increase in wealth. An expense is spending of wealth on things that retain no significant economic value or are consumed. When we "spend" wealth on things that retain substantial economic value, we are not really spending but rather converting our wealth from one form of capital to another.

Consider that under our current law when our portfolio of assets increases in value by say, $30,000, it is not income under the law. But we still see that our wealth has increased, and that makes us feel pretty good. But because the assets have not been sold, no income is realized, and therefore no tax is due.

Most of us don't experience an increase in the value of our portfolio of assets. Most of us don't have a portfolio of assets. And most of us that do experience an increase in the value of our portfolio of assets experience this only in relation to home ownership or our 401(k)s and IRAs. Overwhelmingly, any increase in wealth experienced by most of us comes in major part from earning income by our labor, and to a minor extent, interest on bank deposits. Therefore, more than any other form of taxation, taxes on earned income results in an immediate and substantial diminishment of the individual's or family's ability to accumulate wealth.

Capital gains too are "income" as the term is defined in the law. But capital gains are not an increase in wealth generated through labor but rather by an increase in the value of assets that is realized when those assets are sold. The sale creates the taxable event, unless it is deferred through a mechanism such as the "like kind exchange" provisions of the Internal Revenue Code.

Historically a distinction has been made between short-term and long-term capital gains. Short-term gains have generally been taxed on par with dividend income or interest income, and for much of modern history, on par with or greater than taxes on earned income (through labor). Long-term gain has generally been taxed at substantially reduced rates. In more recent times, all capital gains have received an advantageous tax rate as compared to tax on dividends, interest, or labor.

How does this system of capital gains taxation affect decisions regarding the use of capital?

First, it makes investment in appreciating assets more desirable than investment in dividend or interest paying investments.

Suppose Bill Gates had invested $100,000 in Microsoft stock. That stock could appreciate in value to $100,000,000 or more without a taxable event occurring. In that case, Bill Gates would avoid any tax on that $99,900,000 increase in his wealth. If that increase occurred over twenty-five years, Mr. Gates would have earned the equivalent of compound annual interest at 31.8257%. If he had invested that $100,000 in a mortgage or CD paying 31.8257%, how would he have fared? If he paid the tax at a 30% tax rate and reinvested the 70% of the interest, at the end of twenty-five years, he would have not $100,000,000 but rather only $18,666,185. Why? Because in allowing the return on the value of the stock to compound without having to pay any tax on that return, it allowed a total of $26,523,122 of earnings to go untaxed and to be fully reinvested for Mr. Gates's benefit.

For the specific analysis that explains these numbers, see the table below.

Table 7: Comparative illustration of after tax effect on accumulated wealth growth with stock versus CD or mortgage investment at 31.8257% annual return

Stock	Year	CD or Mortgage	Earned Interest	Reinvest after Tax
$100,000		$100,000	$31,826	$122,278
$131,826	1	$122,278	$38,916	$149,519
$173,780	2	$149,519	$47,585	$182,829
$229,087	3	$182,829	$58,187	$223,560
$301,995	4	$223,560	$71,149	$273,364
$398,108	5	$273,364	$87,000	$334,264
$524,808	6	$334,264	$106,382	$408,731
$691,832	7	$408,731	$130,082	$499,789
$912,012	8	$499,789	$159,061	$611,131
$1,202,267	9	$611,131	$194,497	$747,279
$1,584,896	10	$747,279	$237,827	$913,758
$2,089,301	11	$913,758	$290,810	$1,117,325
$2,754,235	12	$1,117,325	$355,596	$1,366,242
$3,630,790	13	$1,366,242	$434,816	$1,670,614
$4,786,314	14	$1,670,614	$531,685	$2,042,793
$6,309,592	15	$2,042,793	$650,133	$2,497,886
$8,317,664	16	$2,497,886	$794,970	$3,054,365
$10,964,819	17	$3,054,365	$972,073	$3,734,816
$14,454,449	18	$3,734,816	$1,188,631	$4,566,858
$19,054,679	19	$4,566,858	$1,453,435	$5,584,262
$25,118,964	20	$5,584,262	$1,777,231	$6,828,324
$33,113,250	21	$6,828,324	$2,173,162	$8,349,537
$43,651,774	22	$8,349,537	$2,657,299	$10,209,646
$57,544,256	23	$10,209,646	$3,249,291	$12,484,150
$75,858,119	24	$12,484,150	$3,973,168	$15,265,368
$100,000,496	25	$15,265,368	$4,858,310	$18,666,185

Even at less spectacular annual returns, say 12%, the discrepancy perseveres, as the next table shows. You will see that here I compare a mortgage or CD investment that earns interest to a growth stock.

Table 8: Comparative illustration of effect of present tax system on mortgage investment versus investment in nondividend paying stock, each earning 12% per year

Presently			2% Tax on Wealth	
	Mortgage	Stock	Mortgage	Stock
Amount Invested	$100,000.00	$100,000.00	$100,000.00	$100,000.00
Ann. % Return	12%	12%	12%	12%
Yr 1 Gross Return	$ 12,000.00	$ 12,000.00	$ 12,000.00	$ 12,000.00
Tax	$ 3,360.00	$-	$ 2,240.00	$ 2,240.00
Net Return	$ 8,640.00	$ 12,000.00	$ 9,760.00	$ 9,760.00
Balance	$108,640.00	$112,000.00	$109,760.00	$109,760.00
Yr 2 Gross Return	$ 13,036.80	$ 13,440.00	$ 13,171.20	$ 13,171.20
Tax	$ 3,650.30	$-	$458.62	$458.62
Net Return	$ 9,386.50	$ 13,440.00	$ 12,712.58	$ 12,712.58
Balance	$118,026.50	$125,440.00	$122,472.58	$122,472.58
Yr 3 Gross Return	$ 14,163.18	$ 15,052.80	$ 14,696.71	$ 14,696.71
Tax	$ 3,965.69	$-	$548.19	$548.19
Net Return	$ 10,197.49	$ 15,052.80	$ 14,148.52	$ 14,148.52
Balance	$128,223.99	$140,492.80	$136,621.10	$136,621.10
Yr 4 Gross Return	$ 15,386.88	$ 16,859.14	$ 16,394.53	$ 16,394.53
Tax	$ 4,308.33	$-	$610.86	$610.86
Net Return	$ 11,078.55	$ 16,859.14	$ 15,783.67	$ 15,783.67
Balance	$139,302.54	$157,351.94	$152,404.77	$152,404.77
Yr 5 Gross Return	$ 16,716.30	$ 18,882.23	$ 18,288.57	$ 18,288.57
Tax	$ 4,680.57	$-	$681.44	$681.44
Net Return	$ 12,035.74	$ 18,882.23	$ 17,607.13	$ 17,607.13
Balance	$151,338.28	$176,234.17	$170,011.90	$170,011.90
Over 5 Years Taxes Paid	$ 19,964.89	$-	$ 4,539.12	$ 4,539.12

Because of the less spectacular returns, I have used a tax rate of 28%. Then I compare the taxes paid under the Fair Tax System, charging a flat tax of 2% on wealth. The mortgage investor pays nearly twenty thousand dollars in taxes over five years. The stock investor pays no taxes over the same period. You will see that under the Fair Tax System, the investor in the mortgage with a fixed interest return receives a very substantial tax decrease. Also, under the Fair Tax System, each investor pays the same tax. Therefore, the investors' investment decisions will be made solely upon considerations of safety, liquidity, and return, without consideration of taxes.

But one might protest, "What about the tax burden with respect to the stock if the stock is sold after five years?" Well, in that case, the long-term capital gain will equal $76,234.17. Under the current state of the law for long-term gains, the maximum tax will be 15% or 20% depending on the year of sale. At 15%, the tax would be $11,435.12, far less than the $19,964.89 paid by the mortgage investor. Even at 20%, the tax would be only $15,246, 76% of the tax burden imposed upon the investor in mortgages who earned the same income.

Before we leave this topic, let's look at the taxation of the same earned income over the five-year period.

If an unmarried laborer earned only the same return from his labor as the stock investor above, under the current tax system, he would pay $15,263 in taxes, including his portion (1/2) of the social security tax. This is less than the tax illustrated for the mortgage investor above because I assumed that the mortgage investor received all his investment income in addition to his earned income and that therefore I computed his tax on his investment income at 28%. When a laborer earns only that income, his tax is based upon graduated tax rates, different rates that apply to different levels of income beginning at the lowest levels of income that are, except for social security taxes, not taxed at all.

Of course, the argument can be made that the employer paid portion of social security tax is, like the employee's base pay, paid in exchange for the employee's labor, and that therefore the actual tax charged on labor is higher still, about 7.65% higher. Certainly, if someone were self-employed, he or she would have to pay both the employee and employer portions.

Under the Fair Tax System, the laborer would pay no taxes on his income at all, allowing him to either spend the portion now lost to taxes or to save and invest it and start building a net worth. As a net worth is established and grows, it would then be taxed at 2% annually.

People with wealth can and do manage their wealth so that relative to their income, they pay far less in taxes than a coal miner, hotel clerk, shoemaker, or busboy. They do that with the assistance of tax breaks like the mortgage interest deduction, investing in low-budget films which today provides a dollar-for-dollar tax deduction, taking depreciation (phantom expenses) on depreciating assets such as buildings, etc. Relative to their real income, specifically the increase in the value of their portfolio of investments in any year, they pay vastly less in taxes than a laborer. Comparing the taxes paid by the wealthy and the typical laborer who lives largely paycheck to paycheck, the wealthy pay far, far less than the laborer.

Then, too, tax laws can and do subsidize certain recreational and lifestyle pursuits of the wealthy. Travel can often be largely for pleasure, but when linked to business purposes, the cost becomes largely deductible. Thoroughbred farms, a ranch in Montana, private jets, etc. all can be enjoyed while benefiting from tax subsidies. When costs associated with such pursuits obtain tax benefits, these and similar activities, often enjoyed by the wealthy, are subsidized by the rest of us.

The wealthy manage and allocate capital resources to maximize their net after-tax yield. And so the complexity of the tax laws remains a fundamental factor in their decision-making.

Promotion of a Free Market

By applying a small flat tax on wealth, the Fair Tax System encourages the ideals of a "free market" and moves the reality closer to the ideal. Let me repeat that. By applying a small flat tax on wealth, the Fair Tax System encourages the ideals of a "free market" and moves the reality closer to the ideal. That's right. This is crucial to understand.

Contrary to the political rhetoric, we do not have a "free market" now. Free market economics presupposes many sellers and many buyers for any commodity. More and more, there are fewer and fewer sellers of many commodities in our economy. And as the great middle class is squeezed by various economic forces, including but not limited to an unfair tax system that places a tax burden upon them disproportionate to their wealth, there become fewer and fewer buyers with discretionary wealth or income to spend.

Further, in a free market, economic transactions are determined in a marketplace based more purely upon considerations of risk and reward undistorted by tax considerations. To the extent that the tax system favors some at the expense of others, it perverts the ideal of a free market.

Implementing the Fair Tax System, though, will not by itself restore "free market" conditions to our economic system. But it is a necessary component. Without it, we will never really have anything like a free-market economy operating to bring our country economic justice and prosperity.

Free Market—The Buyer Side of the Equation

If implemented, the Fair Tax System will create, almost immediately, larger numbers of people with discretionary wealth and income. In this way, it will go a long way to assuring half of the equation, specifically large numbers of buyers for most products and services. And it will also remove tax considerations from the process of making economic decisions (from buying, selling, and investment decisions). But what about the seller side of the equation?

Antitrust Considerations—The Seller Side of the Equation

We have, in recent history, lived through a time of record numbers of corporate mergers and acquisitions. As a result, there are fewer and fewer sellers of goods and services *vis-à-vis* the consumer market and fewer and fewer buyers of labor *vis-à-vis* the labor market. This trend is inherently anticompetitive and an anathema to the operation of a free market.

Surely, some of this is necessitated by the amount of capital inherently required to be brought to bear in certain economic or industrial pursuits. We can look at history and trace the economic metamorphosis from an economy largely based upon subsistence and local agriculture to one of agribusiness, from an economy based upon consumption of homemade and local made goods and services to the global economy we have today.

As the country pursued its self-proclaimed manifest destiny, it had to build the transportation and communication infrastructure required to tie the vast country together. This required manufacturing techniques and capacity and exploitation of resources on a scale never before attempted. It was in this context that the Fricks, the Morgans, and the Carnegies accumulated the vast industrial fortunes for which they have become known.

In building their economic empires as they did, they looked for ways to bring vast capital resources under centralized control. The corporation is the enterprise that today makes this possible. We are all familiar with it. But initially, it was the "business trust."

A business trust was a form of business entity used in the late nineteenth century with the explicit intent to create a monopoly. Some, but not all, were organized as trusts in the legal sense, and therefore the name "business trust" was used generically. They were created when business leaders convinced (or often coerced) the owners of all the companies in one industry to convey their businesses to a board of trustees in exchange for dividend-paying certificates. The board would then manage all the companies in "trust" for the shareholders and, in the process, minimize or eliminate competition. Eventually the term came to be used to refer to monopolies in general. Prominent trusts included, among others, Standard Oil, US Steel, the American Tobacco Company, and the International Mercantile Marine Company.

The Sherman Antitrust Act was passed and signed into law by President Harrison in 1890. It was named after its author Sen. William Sherman, who later became Secretary of the Treasury under President Harrison. Still later, he became President McKinley's Secretary of State. The act was the first of the laws to become known as antitrust laws in the States or competition laws in Europe.

In 1898, President William McKinley appointed the Industrial Commission, which was in existence until 1902. This executive branch appointed commission ushered in the "trust busting" era of American politics. McKinley, of course, was assassinated in 1901.

Theodore Roosevelt was elected to assume the office of the presidency soon afterward, in 1902. The Sherman Act had not been used in court for many years. Embracing the recommendations of the Industrial Commission, President Roosevelt seized upon the Sherman Act and used it extensively in his administration to break up the major business trusts of the time. Consequently, President Roosevelt became known as the "trust buster."

The Sherman Act remained a useful tool, becoming the primary governmental sword wielded by Roosevelt's successor, President William Howard Taft against the monopolists. Roosevelt's "trust busting" policies were continued under Taft with even more vigor.

The Sherman Antitrust Act is still in existence today. It provides that "[E]very person who shall monopolize, or attempt to monopolize, or combine or conspire with any other person or persons, to monopolize any part of the trade or commerce among the several States, or with foreign nations, shall be deemed guilty of a felony…" The act placed enforcement responsibility upon the government.

The Clayton Antitrust Act was passed in 1914 during the administration of President Woodrow Wilson. It was passed to fix perceived deficiencies with the Sherman Antitrust Act, and today, together with that act, constitute the principal body of US antitrust law.

These antitrust laws were passed, in theory, to prevent monopolies in our society and to outlaw other "unfair business practices" with the intent to preserve a free market. Certainly, not all economists agree with the efficacy or salutary effect of these laws. But regardless of the economic consequences of these laws and their enforcement, generally, our citizenry agree that these protections are needed to preserve a fair market, if not an efficient market.

The point was made by Representative William Mason, congressman from Illinois in 1890, during debate on the law. Answering critics of the law who argued that trusts have made products cheaper and reduced prices, Rep. Mason stated, "Trusts have made products cheaper, have reduced prices; but if the price of oil, for instance, were reduced to one cent a barrel, it would not right the wrong done to people of this country by the trusts which have destroyed legitimate competition and driven honest men from legitimate business enterprise" (Congressional Record, 51st Congress, 1st session, House, June 20, 1890, p. 4100).

Certain industries were given exemptions from these laws because of the nature of those industries, which required enormous investments in capital, and because in these industries, it seemed that having competitors set up separate and parallel infrastructure would be impractical and an enormous waste of resources. Ma Bell, our nationwide phone company, became a classic example, as did our regional utilities and railroads. These exempt monopolies were therefore sanctioned and assured a reprieve from the competitive risks of the marketplace. The cost to them for this exemption was regulation.

For many years, these regulated monopolies were assured a reasonable rate of return to its investors. The virtually guaranteed safety and predictability of investment return attracted large investment from private capital sources. Service of the public interest was assured by and provided through the regulatory bodies that existed to guard against the potential abuses of monopolistic power, while helping to assure a fair return to shareholders.

Another major exemption from the strictures of these antitrust laws was granted to unions. This was necessitated since big business started aggressively using the Sherman Act to sue union organizers and prevent union formation and survival. It was never the intent of the law, though, to apply to the organization of labor and to collective bargaining. So with passage of the Clayton Antitrust Act of 1914, unions were explicitly exempted from the reach of the act.

Organized Labor and the Free and Fair Market

Nevertheless, many large companies became megaliths helped along by access to American private capital markets regulated by the Securities Exchange Commission, such as the New York Stock Exchange or the American Stock Exchange. At the same time, the supply of workers to industry grew enormously, largely due to two factors: (1) massive immigration from abroad, and (2) the movement of large populations out of rural areas to the cities. More and more workers, who really had no bargaining power against the demands of these large employers, fell prey to corporate exploitation of labor. Given the workers' absolute need for employment and their need to compete in labor markets with relatively few suppliers of jobs, they pretty much had to take whatever was offered in terms of pay, benefits, and working conditions.

This reality resulted in many tragic and dramatic examples of the ill effects of corporate dominance over labor in a largely unregulated market. The unequal bargaining position of workers combined with a "who gives a damn about anything but shareholder return and the bottom line" attitude that was endemic to large corporations competing for capital. This created an economic environment ripe for the exploitation of workers. The combination resulted in low wages and terrible working conditions that caused disease, injury, and death to significant populations of workers. After years of well publicized incidents of worker deaths and injuries due to horrendous working conditions and years of the resistance of business to attempts to improve standards through legislative or regulatory action, the political stage was finally dressed to accommodate congressional action.

In 1935, The National Labor Relations Act (or Wagner Act) was passed to assure the right of workers to unionize and to create and legitimize an arsenal of tools at organized labor's disposal in the collective bargaining process. The National Labor Relations Act guaranteed the right of workers to unionize without retaliation by employers and to collectively bargain for better pay, work conditions, and benefits. At their peak, unions were effective at raising the standard of living of its members specifically and of all workers generally, improving workplace safety, and preserving the dignity of labor. Labor unions were largely responsible for the growth of a large middle class in America. With effectively enforced labor laws, workers could wield nearly equal bargaining position with even the largest employers.

The tables turned significantly in favor of the large commercial and industrial interests once again with the enactment of the Taft–Hartley amendments to the National Labor Relations Act of 1947. Sweeping changes were made in US labor law. Taft–Hartley outlawed closed shops and secondary boycotts. It allowed individual states to outlaw union security clauses by passing what opponents of compulsory unionism call "right to work" laws. It required unions and employers to give sixty days' notice before undertaking strikes or other forms of economic action and gave the president authority to intervene in strikes that potentially could create a national emergency. Taft–Hartley excluded supervisors from coverage under the act, required special treatment for professional employees and guards, codified the Supreme Court's earlier ruling that employers have a constitutional right to express their opposition to unions, gave employers the right to file a petition asking the board to determine if a union represents a majority of its employees, and allowed employees to petition to oust their union or to invalidate the union security provisions of any existing collective bargaining agreement. The amendments also involved the federal courts directly in enforcing the secondary boycott provisions of the act by giving employers the right to sue unions for damages caused by a secondary boycott. In other words, after the gains of 1947, the cause of labor suffered a substantial loss of much of the power that had enabled it to stand toe to toe with big businesses.

In 1959, in less sweeping amendments, Congress again amended the law, taking away from unions some other weapons that had been in their arsenals. In 1974, in a small and, since 1947, rare labor legislative victory, Congress extended the act to apply to health care institutions.

Unions have made repeated attempts to obtain legislative amendments to the act to eliminate right-to-work provisions, expand construction unions' right to picket at sites where other building trades employees work, strengthen the protections for employees fired during organizing campaigns, require the National Labor Relations Board to prosecute violations of the act more aggressively, and limit employers' power to hire permanent replacements for strikers. None of those efforts have succeeded.

If you want to learn more detail about trusts, corporations, regulation of monopolies and a related issue, deregulation, I suggest you begin with *An Economic History of the United States* by Ronald E. Seavoy, PhD. Dr. Seavoy is Professor Emeritus of History at Bowling Green State University and, in 2006, published this particular text written for undergraduate courses. Some readers may find it a bit dry, but it provides an excellent survey and more in-depth treatment of the topics discussed here. It also provides an extensive bibliography for further reading on specific topics.

Implications of Media Oligopoly on Control of Elections

The Fair Tax System will not in and of itself reverse the trends that have been favoring monopoly power of industries, industries that now constitute largely unregulated corporate oligopolies. An oligopoly is by definition a market situation in which each of a few producers affects but does not individually control the market. But our experience has shown that oligopolies can and do act informally and implicitly as if they got together to fix prices for goods and services and for the labor they employ. In other words, they effectively control a market without having to enter into formal or even covert informal agreements or conspiracies to restrain trade. Look, for instance, to the oil industry, the automobile industry, steel, or the airlines. Further, globalization has increased the ability of these corporate giants to exploit labor and even national resources.

But for our topic, the Fair Tax System, what is most relevant is the control that the mega commercial and industrial interests exercise over the public discourse in the political arena. This control is exercised in, at least, two ways. They are (1) control over the mainstream media upon which most of the public relies to get information and (2) the dependence of politicians running for high office upon big business for campaign resources and for information.

The way we run our politics, no one gets elected to high office without raising large amounts of private money. Democrats and Republicans alike must largely respond to the demands and concerns of their contributors. So long as "we the people" are content to delegate the responsibility to financially support campaigns for public office, the situation will remain as it is. More and more people express a desire to eliminate the influence of money in politics. They rail against the fact that politicians time and again sell out the public interest in favor of the special interests that provide money, the mother's milk of a political career. But expecting politicians to put public interest first is no more than a fantasy unless we, as a society, are willing to finance campaigns of public officials and either prohibit or disincentivize private political contributions to campaigns. Prohibition would require a Constitutional Amendment since the Supreme Court has ruled that donating money to political campaigns is the equivalent of speech, which is therefore protected by the First Amendment. Disincentivizing private political contributions can only be accomplished by a sufficient commitment to public financing of candidacies so that candidates can reject private contributions and still get elected.

But paying the cost of campaigns is only part of the problem. There is, too, the dependence of our policy makers on special interests for information.

Increasingly the world is a complex and technical place. Policy makers must have information to make decisions. Making good policy depends upon having good information, meaning accurate and unbiased information and analysis. If the voting public placed a desire for good public interest policy as a highest priority, it would insist that policy makers have independent staffs with appropriate expertise adequate to collect and analyze information needed to make law and policy decisions in the public interest. To an extent, legislatures at all levels all over the country have such staffs, but largely on the cheap. Therefore, these staffs are highly dependent upon industries affected by policy and legislation for information.

Making matters worse, when staff members in the halls of government work with an industry on regulation or legislation, there is an unwritten expectation that the industry will offer fat jobs to staff members who accommodate industry desires after these staff members leave government, as they almost inevitably do. Why? Because in comparison to the money and perks that industry throws at them, there is little incentive to stay in government and public service.

When industry spends money to provide information that looks authoritative, it either passes these costs on to consumers (all of us) in the form of higher prices (a hidden tax) or ostensibly takes a hit on its profits. But obviously, in the calculus of these industries, all big businesses, it is worth whatever the cost in that acceptance of their data by legislative and regulatory staffs results in favorable decisions of all sorts.

There are situations, surely, when industries lobby with information prepared by them and that is contradicted by information prepared and presented by countervailing interest groups. But like a jury weighing conflicting expert testimony, the decision maker must choose between these interests and is justified, in theory, in choosing either way based upon whose information it finds to be most credible. This provides ample opportunity for rationalization and for cover since the decision maker can simply look the public in the eye and state that he or she finds the data presented by one side or the other more credible. In these cases, the evaluative process related to conflicting evidence is dangerously affected by the dependence of politicians on private money support for elections, making it likely that the politician will be "honestly influenced" to the point of view of the wealthier and more generous interest.

If one understands the dynamics, it is typically not a fair fight between, for instance, Greenpeace and Big Lumber or Big Agriculture because it takes all the resources Greenpeace can muster just to keep up with the deluge of information and issues and has little if any resources to provide significant financial support to campaigns, or even to deliver votes.

The one-two punch is landed with knockout results with the recent concentration of control of major media outlets by conservative global citizens and mega industries like Time/Warner and Rupert Murdoch's company News Corp. More and more, every outlet is owned or controlled by fewer and fewer individuals, responsive to the demands of fewer people still. This control is so insidious that it can convincingly promote a completely opposite reality, a Bizarro world. Look how effectively and for how long the media has sold the idea of the "liberal press."

No political administration has used this recent trend in media ownership and control better than the administrations of George W. Bush and Donald Trump, or perhaps one should say never has the media so completely influenced the political agenda of any presidency.

So what are the solutions?

Public financing of elections for all public offices, prohibiting private money contributions, directly or indirectly in support of candidates, is one solution. But providing public financing in competitive amounts affords another solution. The details of a fair system to award access to such financing would have to be worked out, of course. But this certainly could be done. There has been some experimentation with publicly financed campaigns on a state level, and to pass constitutional muster, such laws must allow candidates to opt in to public financing with conditions or the opportunity to opt out in favor of private financing. Although these experiments have enjoyed limited success at the local level, they have been less successful at the highest levels of government. At the United States presidential level, public financing of elections exists in theory. But every significant candidate except John Edwards has opted out of public financing because of its limits on spending. Why? Because available private money contributions dwarf the public money offered, even for those candidates like Barak Obama, that for political reasons have opted to refuse PAC (Political Action Committee) money.

Since wealthy interests already finance election campaigns, those same interests can certainly afford to pay taxes in accord with the Fair Tax System, and those taxes could finance campaigns. If wealthy interests were forced to pay a flat tax based upon wealth, perhaps they would be less inclined to contribute substantially to political campaigns.

Necessary First Step to Economic Fairness and Prosperity

The only way, short of amending the Constitution, to make public financing of elections work is to make enough funds available to realistically allow a viable candidate to run an effective campaign and to remain competitive on public money alone. But there is not much public appetite for this solution. Why? Because vested interests revive the boogeyman of higher taxes. The middle class is by now conditioned to expect that higher taxes means higher taxes on the middle-class, a price they do not feel they are able or willing to pay. Because of the structure of our tax system which unfairly burdens the middle class with most of the taxes to be paid, the wealthy preserve a near monopoly on political power and influence that they have been wielding through their money.

Passage of the Fair Tax System would counteract this conditioned response of the middle class. First, the overall tax burden on the middle class would be greatly reduced. Second, the taxes allocable to publicly financed campaigns would be borne by the wealthiest individuals and corporate citizens in direct proportion to their wealth. So the poor and middle class that represent most of the voters could make their voting decisions based upon considerations of sound government policy rather than fears of higher taxes. This would make a workable public campaign finance law politically viable even without a Constitutional Amendment because sufficient funds could be provided by the public to assure the ability of any qualifying candidate to remain competitive in terms of campaign spending with anyone who would choose to run with private contributions instead.

Ironically, the additional revenues needed to finance campaigns would, under the Fair Tax System, still come from the same mon-eyed interests that largely support campaigns now. But because the money would come from collection of taxes, no candidate would be beholden to the interests of the wealthy since qualification for and allocation of the funds would come from the public treasury.

Then, with adequate funds to allow candidates to be truly com-petitive coming from public financing, candidates would have to think twice about refusing public financing and going private. The appearance that such a candidate was trying to buy an office would be independently disastrous to the campaign. In this discussion of public financing of campaigns, I do not mean to foreclose other solu-tions that would reduce the cost of campaigns such as requiring those that use the public airways at little cost to make time available to all viable candidates in time slots that facilitate actual communication with the public. But with the Fair Tax System in place, that would not have to be implemented since sufficient funds would be readily available to buy commercial time at commercial rates. And co-opting use of the public airways might deliberately be rejected by a legisla-ture that operates in the public interest because it might be viewed as a tax "in kind" that would pervert the fairness of the 2% solution. Of course, it is also true that a legislature that is not unduly influenced by corporate interests (and by extension the Federal Communications Commission [FCC]) might well opt to charge market rates for the use of the airways, returning to the treasury additional revenues that could offset the public's cost of campaigns.

The important point is that public financing of campaigns sim-ply won't happen if it adds a billion or two to the cost of a govern-ment that distributes its costs unfairly to an already overburdened middle class. The wealthiest and most powerful individual and cor-porate players know this and take comfort. Why? Because if pol-iticians must rely upon private contributions to campaigns to be elected, the special access of the wealthy is assured. So only by totally reforming the tax system will realistic public financing of elections become palatable to enough voters so that the needed changes in the law can realistically be made.

The Fair Tax System is needed to both (1) make real campaign finance reform coupled with the public financing of candidates for office a politically viable alternative and (2) to allow for the legislation and enforcement necessary to eliminate anticompetitive behavior in the marketplace that the Sherman and Clayton Antitrust laws were enacted to prevent. Achievement of these two goals, facilitated by the Fair Tax System, will launch a new ship of economic fairness and prosperity for our country.

Hopefully, the commonsense approach of the Fair Tax System proposal will have enough appeal to inspire a powerful grass roots movement among voters, who in the final analysis have, but squander, all the power to change the status quo. Nothing short of a powerful grass roots effort will overcome the power of wealth in the political system that benefits from the status quo.

Living Up to Our National Ideals

The Declaration of Independence expresses, perhaps more than any single document, the underlying ideal of the grand American experiment. It justifies the act of revolution with the following language. "We hold these truths to be self-evident, that all men are created equal, that they are endowed by their Creator with certain inalienable Rights, that among these are Life, Liberty and the pursuit of Happiness."

Of course, we have already covered the fact that the reality is far from the ideal in that all persons in our society are not created equal at all. There are advantages of health, wealth, access to education, access to opportunity through family connections, etc.

The proposed fair tax system would tend to level the playing field for everyone.

Through the redistribution of wealth on a regular generational basis, preventing too much wealth and power from becoming concentrated in too few hands, the Fair Tax System makes progress toward creating of us all a family of mankind. Just as no caring parent would afford to one child less opportunity than is afforded to another, all our children, society's children, can be given a more equal opportunity at achieving a good life by our society's adoption and implementation of the Fair Tax System. Just as a loving family cares for its aged and infirm, so too can our society afford benevolence and compassion toward its aged and infirm with implementation of the Fair Tax System.

These benefits would come about not only through the annual per capita tax and an annual flat tax on wealth but also through the redistribution of wealth accomplished by the heavy taxation of (1) large estates and (2) large *inter vivos* (lifetime) gifts. "Large" in this context means gifts that exceed the amount that the body politic decides should be fully available to be passed onto one's children and loved ones and not be taxed at all.

Redistribution of wealth through government would allow for educational and social programs to be made equally available to each of our children, no matter where and to whom they are born. It could provide loving and supportive care to each of our infirm, and to all our aged, many of the benefits of security, dignity, and health care available only to the rich today.

Public funding of parent training programs could help parents to raise children that are psychologically and emotionally healthier. The full funding of early childhood education would allow young minds throughout the country to be stimulated through educational enrichment programs.

With the redistribution of wealth through government, child protective services could be adequately funded, and case workers would have the time and resources to investigate and resolve complaints of suspected serious child abuse or neglect. More children would be able to be rescued by society from abusive circumstances and be afforded the early intervention they need. Such programs would largely prevent the enormous problems and expense to society caused by abused and neglected children who, because of the abuse and neglect, grow up angry and dysfunctional. In the words of Dr. Kerby Alvy, a nationally recognized authority and founder of Center for the Improvement of Child Caring, most people who commit crimes were abused as children. Children who are abused by parents or relatives usually wind up paying us all back for the abuse they suffered, sometimes in obvious ways and sometimes in more subtle ways.

No child need live in poverty. Health and social welfare programs properly funded could provide dignity to all our infirm and aged. The funds available through a heavy taxation of large gifts and estates could also fund those important research and development projects to advance important communal objectives such as alternative energy, pollution control, nanotechnology, and medical advances. The complete list of benefits to society that could result from the systematic redistribution of wealth through government cannot be fully anticipated.

But also, by eliminating the taxation of income and spending (income, social security, Medicare, and sales taxes), families could more easily accumulate wealth and at the same time spend to support our consumer-based economy.

The Global Economy and Free Trade

One of the major issues facing the country today is the displacement of American industries because of globalization and free trade. This has caused, and continues to cause, the loss of whole sectors of the American economy.

One solution, advocated by many well-meaning political commentators, is to increase tariffs to protect American industries and the jobs they support. The use of tariffs or other penalties in response to unfair trade subsidization of local industries by other countries is one thing. It may well be good policy to protect domestic industry from unfair foreign competition, and tariffs maybe a good strategic choice to do so. But a better choice in such cases may well be to simply close access to our markets to countries engaging in unfair competitive practices.

Apart from the unfair subsidization of foreign companies by their governments, either by direct subsidization or by permitting sweat shop exploitation of workers within its borders, it is nevertheless true that some industrial or commercial enterprises can more efficiently be carried on in other parts of the world. In that case, it is best for American industry to cede those industries, unless the industry is necessary for the national defense. Our current resistance to ceding these areas of commerce comes from the displacement of workers caused and the adverse effects on the local economies.

Currently, with large corporate interests exercising effective control over policy in this country, for all the reasons we've already discussed, there certainly will be no abandonment of a general policy of free global trade. But implementation of the Fair Tax System will go a long way to taking care of the problems caused by loss of American jobs overseas.

As discussed elsewhere, the Fair Tax System's implementation is an important step to bringing about the public financing of campaigns for high office, and thereby substantially reducing the voice of corporate interests in the policy debate. Once office holders are no longer held hostage to the need to raise enormous sums in order to get elected and be reelected, they can focus on the public interest.

That doesn't mean that they will ultimately want to bring back tariffs and economic protectionism. Free trade may well be a worthy goal for the United States and the world, so long as the short-term pain the transition causes can be ameliorated and the long-term benefits to society maximized.

One of the enormous benefits of the Fair Tax System is that there will be substantially more funds available to deal with society's problems caused by free trade and a global economy. The displacement of workers and the loss of industries is a problem from at least two points of view. First, workers' lives are terribly disrupted, and their economic security is seriously jeopardized. Second, if we become totally dependent upon other countries to provide goods and services in necessary industries like steel and oil, we become hostage to our needs on the world stage.

The latter concern is ameliorated by the Fair Tax System because we will be able to pay off the national debt, placing a priority on paying the debt to foreigners. This will make our society much less vulnerable to inappropriate foreign pressures. Also, we must recognize, that if we focus on bringing the human and capital resources of this country to bear upon the things we do best, and in areas in which we can remain competitive in a world marketplace, we will be able to stand toe to toe with any country in trade issues and enforce our fair-trade demands.

As to the first issue, the loss of jobs and the economic pain caused to those families affected, the Fair Tax System will provide more than sufficient tax revenues to maintain a safety net, while adequately funding the retraining and reeducation programs needed to move displaced workers into new economically productive jobs and enterprises, at least comparable to those positions they lost. Further, if these corporate interests that are moving the jobs out of the country are required to pay their fair share of the societal cost of maintaining these remedial programs, i.e., the safety net, retraining and reeducation, then, for them, the cost benefit calculus will change, and they will likely slow the process for reasons of self-interest.

The Fair Tax System and the revenues it provides will allow us to provide some sort of taxpayer funded national health system. By placing the burden for health care on the body politic rather than upon employers and individuals, keeping businesses of all sorts in the United States will become significantly easier. The cost to the companies who stay will be reduced by the billions they now spend to provide health benefits and process payroll withholding for current workers and for retired workers and their families. Thus, American companies will be able to be more competitive in world markets.

The challenge of a global economy is only partly met by providing adequate safety net programs for families of workers who through job exportation lose their job and can't find work in their occupation. Even providing well-funded job retraining programs for such programs does not fully meet the challenge. The well-being of our nation and its citizens also depends upon establishing the industries here at home that will become the major exports of the future.

The government funding provided by the Fair Tax System can be used to seed the technologies that will become the service and manufacturing jobs here that will enable us to compete favorably in the global economy.

The case for the need for such programs is made convincingly in Thomas L. Friedman's book, *The World Is Flat: A Brief History of the Twenty-First Century*. But no viable solution is offered there as to how the cost of these programs will be paid.

Home Ownership

The Fair Tax System will bring home ownership and ownership of investment real estate into the lives of more and more people. Real estate will be taxed on equity only, and since government borrowing would be eliminated or minimized, it will make capital for mortgages available at much lower interest rates. The consequent real property tax savings and mortgage interest savings will allow for an increase in the pace of equity buildup. The last statement may not be intuitively obvious, so let me offer an example.

Borrowing the numbers developed and presented in *A Comprehensive Analysis of Westside Park*, Part I, of an *Exploratory Study to Establish a Special Improvement District on Springfield and South Orange Avenues, Newark, New Jersey; Report to the Corinthian Housing Development Corporation and New Community Corporation* (May 11, 1998), let's assume that real property taxes are 3.9% of fair market value of a home.

If a family with a good income buys a house in a Newark suburb for $750,000, the property tax burden on that house will be $29,250 per year. If the family buys the house with $250,000 down, the family has equity of only $250,000 but is still paying $29,250 per year in property tax. Assuming that under the Fair Tax System wealth were taxed at 2%, the tax on equity would be $5,000 per year. This would afford the family an additional $24,250 per year to be used for savings, investment, and for purchase of consumer goods and services.

The size of a mortgage loan for which a buyer can qualify is a function of his or her family income relative to housing related expenses. About 1/3 of one's income can reasonably be allocated to housing for the purpose of mortgage underwriting. For these purposes, interest, amortization, taxes, and insurance are counted as payment for housing. Savings of $24,250 per year on taxes allows a much bigger mortgage to be obtained by the family that would buy the $750,000 property, making the house available to those families with a much lower down payment.

Ownership of real estate would thus be made more accessible to more families of modest incomes since homes could be purchased with smaller down payments. Also, if mortgage rates were lower because of the decreased demand for borrowing caused by the absence of government from the market as a borrower, dollar for borrowed dollar payments on mortgages would be lower still.

The stated objectives of virtually every administration in government include the promotion of programs to increase the percentage of citizens that enjoy home ownership. No other program in our history would have so profound an impact on home ownership than would implementation of the Fair Tax System. It would allow families to accumulate down payments much faster. It would allow them to buy with lower down payments. It would substantially lower interest rates and property taxes. It would make ownership of real estate possible for millions and millions of American families who are essentially priced out to the market today.

It is, of course, true that the entry of so many perspective buyers would initially create an upward pressure on prices of real estate, but the elimination of the tax advantages of home ownership would decrease demand relative to renting and have a countervailing effect on prices. Also, the increase in demand due to more people being able to buy would stimulate building and create downward pressure on housing prices and create the prosperity that comes with it.

In any case, the prices of homes would more accurately reflect free market conditions.

Creation of Jobs

Job creation in our economy is largely dependent upon the ability of the poor and middle class to afford to spend for consumer goods and services. Wealthy families spend a much smaller percentage of their incomes and assets for consumer goods and services than do the poor and middle class because one can only consume so much.

The poor and middle class are prevented from consuming more goods and services, not because of lack of desire or need for these goods and services but because without sufficient wealth, they can rely only upon their paycheck or funds provided to them through public assistance, credit cards, and growing personal debt. With no taxes being taken from their paychecks, there is a stronger incentive to work and greater capacity to spend, save, and invest.

Disappearance of the Underground Economy

With taxes based upon income, individuals are given powerful incentive to dissolve into an artesian well of a cash economy. That incentive disappears under the Fair Tax System.

First, since income is not taxed, there is no disincentive to earn visible income. Working "under the table" will become a thing of the past.

Second, at a tax equal to 2% of net worth, there is little if any incentive to keep assets in cash hidden under the mattress, figuratively speaking. Nor is there sufficient disincentive to save and invest and thereby to build a net worth. But what about the proverbial person who is inclined to cut off his nose to spite his face? How many people would so hate paying taxes that they would rather avoid taxes than accumulate some savings and investment? Would they prefer instead to take a vow of poverty or hoard those few assets they could in the very few forms that are relatively invisible? Of course, these questions are rhetorical. Such iconoclasts could only realistically choose to (1) spend what they earn or (2) be content to live frugally under social welfare programs and maximize nonwork activities that are available for free or for very little expense. The first choice, spending all they earn, can be fun, at least for a while. Such spending, meanwhile, will support the wealth and well-being of others and will represent a net societal gain. If that choice is made by any individual, it is not a drag on society. The latter choice is not so fun. If social welfare programs are created and managed to be truly for the needy and not those who are needy by choice, the difficulties, benefits, and risks of living under them will be too great for those who do not really need them, especially when considered against the fact that earned income is not taxed. While one can certainly make a case for the benefits of choosing to maximize free or inexpensive nonwork activities, few are predisposed by personality or temperament to recreate away most of their lives in nonspending activity.

It's true, under the Fair Tax System, the Bill Gates and the Elon Musks of the world would pay a lot more in taxes, but it cannot seriously be contended that they would rather be poor than pay such a large tax bill.

CHAPTER 6

✧ ✧ ✧

Possible Disadvantages?

Well, you might think that "all sounds pretty good, but there must be disadvantages of the Fair Tax System."

Based upon years of informal discussions with several people from various walks of life, here are the commonly perceived arguments advanced against making the change.

"Double Taxation" Argument

This point of view is theoretical and heard, in my experience, from the WWII generation. It goes something like this: "I've worked all my life and paid my taxes on my income. Frugality and sound judgment have allowed me to accumulate some assets, and now you are talking about taxing me again on the same money. This is double taxation." The argument is fallacious for a number of reasons.

First, double taxation is taxation of the same "earnings" at two levels.

One common example is taxation of earnings at the corporate level and then again at the shareholder dividend level. This is routinely done now in our tax system as it exists today. And it is justified by the fact that corporations are separate legal entities that enjoy many benefits of that separateness under the law, as do their shareholders.

Another example is the taxation of foreign investment returns in the country of origin and then again in the hands of the American citizen who made the investment. Many countries have signed agreements to prevent this latter type of double taxation.

Taxing of income was a political choice made by that generation. They can hardly now be heard to complain that it paid taxes on income it chose to tax. It was their choice. There was never, nor could ever there be any "deal" that once income taxes were paid that the resultant net-after-tax income invested and accumulated would never be subject to another tax. By the logic of this argument, after-tax income that is used to acquire, say, real estate would be subject to double taxation when property taxes are assessed on the real estate.

Second, the argument misconstrues the relationship of that generation to their assets and society. It presupposes that somehow in the natural order of things, they would be able to maintain and preserve their accumulated wealth without the protection of our organized society. As we have already discussed, nothing could be further from the truth.

The rationale of that generation for the yearly taxation on the value of real estate is that the owner enjoys every year the services of fire departments, roads providing ingress and egress, zoning and planning, building code enforcement, etc. But the same principle can be seen to be at work to justify the proposed tax on net worth of whatever kind. As already established, as people get older, they are naturally less capable of preserving their wealth from the designs of would be predators. They can enjoy their wealth, day in and day out, only because society provides laws and enforcement of those laws through various means.

Owners of assets enjoy these benefits of society every year. Paying a small tax on the net value of their wealth has them paying a fair pro rata cost of the machinery of government that allows them to keep and enjoy the security and peace of mind their wealth provides in their "golden years." This is fair and equitable proposition.

"Undue Hardship" Argument

Some argue against the Fair Tax System proposal based upon the specter of old people losing their homes as a result.

This is obviously not a big concern because presently homeowners pay 1%–3.5% of the gross value of their homes in property taxes. To the limited extent that such fears are reality based for a few, they threaten to become the tail that wags the dog. It would be relatively few such seniors that would be threatened with losing their homes. It is true that seniors are more likely than young people to own their homes free and clear of a mortgage, and therefore under the Fair Tax System, they would have to pay more taxes on the same house than a young family. But at 2% of the real value of the house, the overall tax burden to the senior involved would likely be less than the combined property tax, sales taxes, and other taxes that the affected senior is already paying.

For those few, if any, for which the expressed fear proved to be reality based, it would be an easy matter for society to craft a remedy. It could, for instance, allow such individuals to defer the payment of all or a portion of their taxes until death, charging a reasonable interest on the amount deferred, which the taxpayer could either pay annually or which could be added to the principal tax debt. Of course, the tax debt in such a case would be a lien against the home which would have to be paid before title to the real estate could be transferred. Basically, society could enjoy a mortgage on the residences of such people due and payable upon the transfer of the asset.

The development of the "reverse mortgage" over the last twenty years presents another solution. Let's consider a senior with a residence worth $600,000. Taxes would be roughly $12,000 per year. If that senior could not afford the tax payments, he or she could take a reverse mortgage to pay all or a portion of the $12,000 per year. As the balance of the loan accrued, the equity in the house would decline, lowering the tax payment each year. Since the escalating balance of the reverse mortgage debt would be an asset in lender's hand, the total tax paid to society would be the same. Each dollar of taxes lost by applying the tax rate against the shrinking equity value of the home would be made up by applying the same tax rate against the growing asset of the mortgage debt in the portfolio of the lender.

"Communism" Argument

Some would argue against the gift and estate tax element of the Fair Tax System based on the premise that the systematic redistribution of wealth through taxation is communism, and therefore an anathema to our values. This, though, is the protestation of the uninformed.

Communism is the ownership of the means of production by the government. The Fair Tax System can be fully implemented without government ownership of the means of production. What government should own or not own is a political decision independent of the means of raising revenue for the government to support its policies and programs. The following argument is closely related to this.

"Destruction of the Free Market" Argument

"America has built its freedom and prosperity on a free market, and your fair tax system will destroy the free market," goes the objection. Another variation is "America is based upon capitalism, and your proposal would destroy the built-in incentives of capitalism which have created our wealth and standard of living."

Tax policy, as it exists, sharply skews the "free market" in which America and the West take so much pride. Just ask any economist and review again the sections on the free market in the previous chapter. Whenever a sufficiently large number of buyers and sellers are in the marketplace, price is determined freely by the market.

A flat tax on wealth removes taxation from the market forces equation. Economic decisions made under a fair tax system are thus made more purely upon free market considerations. The key to a "free market," once tax skewing is removed, will be regaining the political will to publicly finance campaigns for public office, to enforce antitrust laws, reasonably support organized labor, dissemble the oligopoly control of the media, and regulate true monopolies that should be operating in the public interest.

Supreme Court Chief Justice John Marshall in 1819 wrote, "The power to tax involves the power to destroy." Taxation, therefore, distorts the free market. A small tax on all wealth distorts the market the least, if at all. Economic decisions would, under such a system, be made without reference to tax incentives and penalties. The move to a fair tax system would bring the "market" much closer to the ideal of free market economics.

Capitalism is a system in which the productive capital of society is owned by individuals, not governments. It is, if you would like, the opposite of communism. The periodic redistribution of wealth, the third principal of the Fair Tax System, may have socialist leanings, but socialism and capitalism are not inconsistent. The European democracies are more "socialist" than are we, yet still capitalistic. And they are certainly as democratic. Nothing in this proposal would remove capital from private interests and private decision-making. Just the rules would change. Ownership of capital would become necessarily more democratized.

"Destruction of Tax Incentive Policies" Argument

This is just the reverse of the "destruction of the free market" argument.

Some argue that tax incentives are an important tool of social engineering, and that society should not deprive itself of its utility. This argument wrongly assumes that tax incentives are the only or best way to encourage certain economic decisions.

Tax breaks to encourage research and development do serve a purpose. But this purpose can be better served by direct government subsidization of research and development in appropriate cases. Under a tax incentive approach, all research and development is subsidized, even such R&D projects in which the risk/reward calculus would justify the expenditure without consideration of any government subsidy. In such cases, tax subsidization simply amounts to corporate welfare. Tax policy is at best an indirect and inexact way of moving resources to areas of spending or investment that society deems worthwhile. Direct subsidy policies determined by legislatures and regulatory bodies freed from the controlling influence of big business are far more certain, controllable, and effective in furthering the public interest.

Destruction of Charitable Giving in America

Tax breaks are thought to encourage charitable giving and therefore to be a net benefit to society through the enterprise of charitable institutions. But the bulk of charitable contributions are made by many small individual donors who donate in small amounts. Most charitable contributions are motivated by charity, not tax incentives. There has been a great deal of study and analysis in this area.

One of the most interesting and complete, though technical, is *Federal Tax Policy and Charitable Giving* by Charles T. Clotfelter, a study sponsored by the National Bureau of Economic Research and published by the University of Chicago Press in 1986. In his scholarly work, the author points out that tax policy affects giving to some degree based (1) on availability of the tax deduction and (2) on the discounted value of the dollar donated. Both are considerations that influence charitable giving. But while these have an effect, they are not the primary motive for giving.

His work shows that to the extent that a tax effect on charitable giving exists, it is not simply because the deduction allows that the contribution is cheaper after tax (for example $10 given to charity may cost the donor only $8 after considering tax savings), but it is also affected by the amount of discretionary income left to the donor after his taxes are paid. The more discretionary income individuals have, the greater the contributions. Interestingly, statistics show that wealthy people as a group donate less proportionately to their income and their wealth than the middle class.

Therefore, one might expect some, though little, decrease in charitable giving due to the loss of the charitable deduction. But with the Fair Tax System leaving far more income in the pockets of the middle class, it also might increase charitable giving. Of course, no one will know until the move to the Fair Tax System occurs.

To the extent that charitable giving is motivated by tax savings, such tax breaks merely allow those taxpayers to direct how money they would otherwise have paid in taxes will get used. For wealthy taxpayers, they obtain additional advantages at taxpayer expense. They obtain the social and economic benefits of being viewed by society as being philanthropic. They buy themselves the additional social and business contacts that "giving" on a large scale engenders. And to the extent that they retain control over their charitable enterprises, such as through setting up private charitable foundations or directed funds in community foundations, they obtain the myriad of benefits of being able to control the use of great wealth.

Let's look at an example. Bill Gates gave billions to a charitable foundation over which he and his wife retained control. Only a small portion of the funds in the foundation are spent to provide social services in various areas of the economy, both in the US and abroad. The rest is invested, the investments controlled by the Gates. There is an old saying that "possession is nine tenths of the law." And control of wealth is 90% of ownership. Through setting up and controlling charitable foundations, the rich retain most of the benefits of ownership and obtain tax deductions to apply against current and/or future income. They buy the benefits of philanthropy at our expense.

If the United States government through its body politic considers the type of spending elected to be done by the Bill and Melinda Gates Foundation desirable, it can do so itself. And the enormous tax savings to the Gates, through the movement of approximately $80 billion into the Bill and Melinda Gates Foundation, can be recouped by the Treasury and spent on those programs that society collectively decides are important.

Unless we are prepared to let every individual direct the use of his or her tax payments, why should that benefit be accorded to the mega-rich?

"Change Will Cost Too Much" Argument

It's true that every change in the way we do things has an initial cost. But with the Fair Tax System, the cost of collecting taxes at all levels would be sharply reduced in very short order. This would decrease the overall cost of government and allow more of the taxes we collect to go toward productive or life-enhancing things that government can do if it has the resources.

One bureaucracy is all that would be needed to collect taxes and revenues, not the literally thousands that we have today. Procedures could be standardized and systematized in ways that are impossible today. Information obtained on tax returns would be able to be correlated to other records of government and business to improve detection of any attempts at tax cheating. Though relatively few people or entities would have much incentive for significant cheating, those that would want to cheat would have the hardest time hiding or significantly undervaluing assets. Living, as we do now, in a time of the easy electronic flow and correlation of information, enforcement would be simplified. Exactly what do I mean by that?

Public traded securities

An enormous amount of the taxable wealth in the United States, and the world, is in form of publicly traded securities. These are the NASDQ, the New York Stock Exchange, and The Chicago Board of Trade, to name the most significant. Everything is traded on these exchanges from common stocks, preferred stock, bonds, T-Bills, municipal bonds, to commodities such as coffee, copper, steel, and pork.

All those companies represented on the exchange regularly report all aspects of their business life to the public through the Securities and Exchange Commission. The wealth of these companies might be viewed from the perspective of company reporting, which typically reports the book value of appreciating assets rather than their real value. The discrepancy is made worse not just because the company does not show appreciation in value of these assets but also because many of these assets are depreciable for tax purposes, so the asset is carried on the books at a value equal to the purchase price minus the depreciation taken each year.

But the better and more accurate way of determining the value of those companies' assets is by looking at the total number of outstanding equity shares of various types and then multiplying the price per share by the number of shares issued and outstanding, arriving at an enterprise value. This will automatically adjust for good will, the impact of the quality of management, the value of trademarks, patents and copyrights, and the real value of those assets which are accounted for in the corporation's annual report only in terms of book value.

According to its 2006 Annual Report, as of January 31, 2007, Exxon Mobil Corporation, the largest of the Fortune 500 companies traded on the NYSE had 5,693,398,774 shares of common stock outstanding. At the typical 2006 price of about $82 per share, the value of the company was $ 466,858,699,468 (that's $466 billion).

There are some other classes of equity securities outstanding other than common stock, but for the sake of simplicity and to illustrate the point, I will assume there are no other equity shares outstanding.

This means that under the Fair Tax System, Exxon Mobil Corporation would have paid the federal government $9,337,173,989.36 in taxes in 2007 for the 2006 tax year. You might be interested to know how that compares with the taxes it did pay. According to its annual report, Exxon Mobil Corporation paid approximately $100,676,000 of US and non-US taxes, including income and sales-based taxes, in the year 2006 (*Exxon Mobil Corporation Annual Report*, page 17).

As you can see, under the Fair Tax System, Exxon Mobil would have paid about $9.227 billion more in taxes to the US. This is only 2% of its net worth and about 24% of its pre-tax profit for the year. Parenthetically, under the Fair Tax System, its profit for the year would have been even greater than it was because of the savings in the cost of personnel related the elimination of withholding taxes and perhaps for other reasons as well.

Most publicly traded securities are traded on public exchanges and are held in the house name of various institutions. It would be easy to require these institutions to report the names, social security numbers, and valuation determined on a "valuation day" of the portfolio of securities held for the beneficial owners of securities. All the information is already required to be in their computers. This information then can be correlated to taxpayer's returns.

As to the Exxon Mobil Corporation stock, the tax on the net value of the accounts that hold the stock would result in payment to the federal treasury of another $9,337,173,989.36, representing 2% of the value of all that Exxon Mobil stock, from all the various owners of the stock.

That totals almost $19 billion in taxes just from Exxon Mobil Corporation and the owners of its shares. I would guestimate that no more than $250,000,000 was paid in taxes from those sources. But there is no way to know for sure.

I bet you paid in taxes and government fees in that year a lot more than 4% of your net worth.

Private companies (All types)

Private companies must document their existence in many ways. There are almost always government filings needed just to do business. As to many of these required filings, if they are not made, the business is precluded from being able to access the courts, from opening bank accounts in the name of the business, etc. If banks and other financial institutions were required to report the names and taxpayer IDs of its business banking customers, which certainly is required to be done today if any interest or earnings on accounts are paid, with computerization the IRS can easily compare this data against its list of filed returns.

The methods of appraising companies are well-known to economists and CPAs that specialize in this area. Also, there are a plethora of Revenue Rulings and Technical Advice Memoranda from the IRS that shed light on the issue.

Private companies are valued just like publicly held companies in that the value consists of the total of all the assets of the business less the liabilities, including consideration of tangible and intangible assets and liabilities. With public companies, the market for the stock is made by the public acting with information available from SEC filings and helped by analysts working for publishers and stock brokerage houses. At any time, the value of a public company is the total value of all the equity shares in the company.

Private companies do not offer and trade shares in public markets. They are generally valued based upon the revenue and expense history for the business. Generally private companies sell for a price that is a certain multiple of the pretax gross profit of the previous year or of an average of the recent years. The multiplier is often industry specific. These figures are tracked by analyzing actual sales data and then used by appraisers to appraise the value of a business.

With private companies, often ownership is split between "partners" and/or family members. It is well established that controlling interest is worth something in and of itself, a premium. What I mean is this. Take the simple case of a business owned by two partners, A and B. A owns 60% of the business, and B 40%. If the value of the business is $1MM, A's interest is worth more than $600K, and B's interest less than $400K. That's because A has controlling interest. Again, for valuation purposes, there are published Revenue Rulings upon which taxpayers, or their representatives, can rely in making these valuation decisions. But how they make the valuation between them makes no difference under the Fair Tax System. Why? Because so long as 100% of the value of the company is reported and 2% on that value paid, it matters not which taxpayer makes the payment. So in the scenario described, the total taxes paid by the company would be $20,000 per year (2% of $1MM) and $20,000 would be paid by the partners, which could be paid 60%–40% or any way they chose without loss of tax revenue. If you think about it, you can probably see that this $1MM business and its owners, unlike Exxon Mobil Corporation, are probably paying more in total taxes and government fees now than they would be required to pay under the Fair Tax System.

Real estate

To some extent, county tax assessor offices have access to records of each sale of real estate and of every significant improvement of real estate or partition of real estate, among others. A lot of real estate of all types is valued for commercial, financing, or refinancing reasons by qualified real estate appraisers. It would be an easy thing to require these appraisers to electronically report their valuations and thereby be able to maintain a more complete database and history.

When loan applications are submitted, either for mortgages or simply sometimes for personal or business credit lines, the owner of real estate is asked to provide a value for their real estate and the amount of debt. The government could require that the data from these applications be reported to the IRS by banks and lenders, and the data can then be cross-checked against taxpayer returns.

Patents and copyright

A patent or copyright is frequently owned by the inventor or creator directly. Whoever owns these rights, the value of a patent or copyright is calculated very much like a private business since any-one buying the intellectual property would be buying the stream of income that comes with ownership. Anyone making payments to the owner of such intellectual property can be required to report the identity and taxpayer ID number of the recipient of the income. Again, this information can be electronically checked against returns.

Fine jewelry, art, and collectibles

Fine jewelry, art, and collectibles off all kinds are bought and sold not only for use but often as an investment asset. The over-whelming majority of such purchases are from dealers of some kind. These dealers will be anxious to report the sale so that they are no longer paying taxes on the value of that inventory. When such things are purchased from abroad, most of these items can be registered as property owned by the new owner at its entry into this country.

The industry keeps abreast of the purchases and sales, and qualified appraisers determine the value of jewelry, art, and collectibles all the time. People that own these investments obtain these appraisals to support the claimed value for insurance purposes. These same appraisals, those used to support the listed value in insurance policies, can support the valuation for tax purposes.

Automobiles

These fall into two categories, transportation and collectibles. In the latter case, the discussion in the previous paragraph applies. In the former, there are a number of authoritative sources available to help a taxpayer determine the value of his or her vehicles, Kelley's Blue Book, being the best known.

If you go through the exercise of trying to think of every kind of asset of significant value, you will see for yourself that nearly all can be tracked into the hands of the owner, especially today with the aid of computerization.

More benefits

There would also be enormous savings to business and individuals in terms of simplifying their tax compliance.

Right now, retail businesses have to collect and pay sales taxes. The expenses to those businesses associated with that activity would be saved. Most businesses in the country have to keep track of inventory and/or property used in business now. If they had to pay taxes on the reported value, there would be no more cost imposed to do the counting.

Many businesses must compute *ad valorem* taxes calculated on the amount of value their process adds to a product. Under the Fair Tax System, such accounting practices and the associated expense could be entirely abandoned. Businesses that employ workers have to spend considerable resources to comply with payroll withholding laws. Those costs too would be saved. No social security taxes, unemployment taxes, etc. would have to be computed, paid, and reported by business, making our businesses more competitive in world markets.

State government agencies assess and collect real property taxes, income taxes, *ad valorem* taxes, disability income taxes, unemployment insurance taxes, business property taxes, motor vehicle registration fees, driver's license renewal fees, park use fees, etc. A move to the Fair Tax System would eliminate all the associated expenses at the state and local levels and most of the expenses related to tax law compliance at the level of private enterprise.

I'm sure, if you ever paid a toll at a bridge or a tunnel, you thought at one time or another like I have. How stupid it is to have to pay people to stand at the toll and collect money, to have to buy machines to collect the money, and to have to pay repair people to repair the machines that collect the money. How much does it cost simply to collect the money? Isn't there a better way? Well, the better way is the Fair Tax System. Under the Fair Tax System, all these unnecessary expenditures would be eliminated.

Again, what is the net result? Businesses would be more profitable, creating more wealth and a greater tax revenue base. Government would spend less on administrative infrastructure and more on productive programs. And either we could constructively spend what we collect in taxes on public interest programs such as infrastructure building and maintenance, police, schools, higher education, emergency response, or health care, to name just a few areas that could benefit from more funding; or we could proportionately lower the tax burden for everyone. Or both.

"Tax Fraud Will Increase" Argument

Many of the taxes we currently collect are largely dependent upon voluntary compliance with tax laws. No one knows the full extent of lost revenues due to tax cheating in the United States, but that the amount is huge is without doubt. This fact adds substantially to the unfairness of the tax system with respect to those who do voluntarily comply with tax laws.

Perhaps the most understood and recognized area of tax cheating is in the world of the underground or cash economy. We have already touched on this in the previous chapter.

A recent article on the cash economy appeared in Barron's Online on January 3, 2005. The headline of this article by Jim McTague reads, "*Going Underground: The shadow economy is about to top $1 trillion—at a great cost to many.*"

According to the article, "If the IRS could collect all the taxes it says that it is owed from the underground economy in a given year, then the current budget deficit would disappear overnight. And if the IRS could collect these taxes every year, then the nation would have surpluses as far as the eye can see."

But the shadow economy is only the most understood area of tax cheating. There are many other examples of how the complexity of the tax system today makes it easy for people to cheat on their taxes. One example that may come as a surprise to many is found and explained in a *New York Times* article dated January 24, 2005, by David Cay Johnston. He reports on the problem as follows:

> "Investors, entrepreneurs and landlords annually avoid paying at least $29 billion in taxes by overstating the price of stocks, businesses and real estate," two professors say in an article being published today in Tax Notes, an influential tax policy journal.
>
> Claiming to have paid more than the actual price for a stock, business, apartment building or piece of art results in a smaller profit being reported when the asset is sold, and a lower tax on that profit.
>
> An unpublicized problem of crisis proportions is plaguing the tax system, one that will cost

the government at least $250 billion in the coming decade...

The potential for abusive reporting in this area, particularly for stocks, "is virtually unlimited," according to the authors, who outline five ways that the law encourages cheating. They added that opportunities to cheat also abound in investment real estate, "where tax-free, like-kind exchanges are increasingly common."

The August 1, 2006, article published in the *New York Times* under the same byline presents yet another example and attempts to quantify the cost to American taxpayers. "So many superrich Americans evade taxes using offshore accounts that law enforcement cannot control the growing misconduct, according to a Senate report that provides the most detailed look ever at high-level tax schemes."

Then Mr. Johnston quantifies the size of the problem. "Cheating now equals about 7 cents out of each dollar paid by honest taxpayers, as much as $70 billion a year, the report estimated."

What's the incentive for sending assets offshore? Mr. Johnston provides the following examples.

Mr. Johnson, known as Woody [the billionaire owner of the New York Jets], told Senate investigators two weeks ago that to buy the Jets in 1999 he had to sell assets, incurring the 20 percent tax on long-term capital gains in effect at the time. He said that a way to defer the tax was proposed by...his accountant at KPMG [a big 8 accounting firm] until he joined Quellos, where he worked closely with Chuck Wilk, a tax lawyer.

The report details a scheme created for Mr. Saban [the billionaire media mogul] to avoid more than $300 million in taxes from sale of his half interest in the Family Channel and related properties. Mr. Saban told Senate investigators

that he never understood the transactions but
undertook them after asking two questions of
Mr. Wilk and his personal tax lawyer, Matthew
Krane.

These costs, of course, must be made up by heavier taxation on the poor and middle class today or, as the result of government borrowing and deficit spending, in the future.

One can see the fraud argument against the Fair Tax System is specious.

The choice is not one as between a tax system without fraud or one with fraud. It is one between a tax system with powerful incentives for massive fraud at all levels or one in which fraud is more difficult and makes little economic sense. Tax fraud in the Fair Tax System would be much less likely to occur because of the low flat rate of tax assessed against net worth.

"No Incentive to Save or Invest" Argument

Almost everyone knows what they are worth financially and would have no real difficulty reporting their net worth through an annual return. Those with more would, of course, have more complex returns, but those with more already require the ongoing services of financial service professionals that are doing the bulk of the work of bookkeeping, evaluating, accounting, and reporting for them.

People with wealth are always updating their financial statements for credit and other reasons. There would, therefore, be no marginal increase in accounting and bookkeeping costs to any taxpayer. In fact, there would probably be some savings because there would be no loopholes to analyze, utilize, and abuse by the schemes of highly paid tax professionals.

As already discussed, a hidden cash economy would be much smaller, if it persisted at all, since assets are much harder to hide than income. Plus there are economic disincentives to hiding wealth because both one's self-interest in obtaining and maintaining credit and one's capacity to put one's wealth to work are dependent upon being able to verify wealth.

Incentives for tax cheating are virtually a nonissue when all taxes are assessed as a small flat rate charged against the net value of one's assets.

Who would cheat? Would a family of four with a net worth of $100,000? An immigrant family with a net worth of $1,500. The former would pay only $600–800 per year (@ $150–200 for each member of the family), plus a small percentage of its net worth at, say, 2% or another $2,000. That family is paying a lot more now with sales taxes, property taxes, income taxes, etc. The family with a $1,500 net worth would pay the same $150–200 for each family member, plus only $30 in taxes on the family's net worth.

As for wealthy individuals, what could be hidden? Publicly traded stock is public. Real estate is real estate, mortgages are recorded, secured loans are secured and filed of record to protect the collateral, and unsecured loans would be documented to assure proof upon default and would be reported by the debtor so as to accurately compute the debtor's net worth for tax purposes. Also, it would be easy to change the law to require notes to be reported from their inception; otherwise, the lender would be precluded from enforcing the obligation to pay through our system of justice.

Cars, boats, and planes are registered and typically insured. Large jewelry or art sales can be reported by the seller, and they will happily report the sale since a failure to report would result in the seller being taxed on the value of inventory no longer in the seller's ownership. Further, such things would likely be itemized with insurers for the purpose of insuring against theft or destruction.

Families might still move assets into trusts, or other legal entities, for reasons of privacy, separation of management from ownership, raising of additional capital, protection from creditors, probate avoidance, or other reasons; but the move would not avoid tax since those entities would be taxed to the same extent as any legal person and the families would be taxed on the value of their interest in the entity, effectively and appropriately doubling the tax. If the device that was elected to be used were not worth the extra tax, then the beneficial owners don't have to use the devices. Since those benefits are only available through the support of the social order anyway, the "double taxation" is justified by the rationale of the Fair Tax System.

No longer would the decision to incorporate small business be motivated by tax incentives related to the deductibility of certain expenses to corporations since corporate income would not be taxed. Corporations could retain capital for future needs without fear of heavy tax penalties now imposed on excess retained dividends. In fact, corporations would have economic incentive to distribute unneeded cash reserves to shareholders to avoid having the value of that cash taxed twice, once in the corporation and once in the value of the shares in the hands of the shareholders.

Establishment of family trusts would be predicated upon considerations of wealth management and distribution of income to family members as needed or desired, not tax considerations.

Charitable trusts would be predicated upon charitable intent, not tax deductions. Community foundations would continue, if at all, because of the long-term advantages of professional management and bona fide charitable intent, not tax motivations.

Limited liability companies (LLCs), real estate investment trusts (REITs), mutual funds, limited partnerships (LPs), and any and every other business or investment entity would be created and maintained for business reasons unrelated to tax avoidance. None of these vehicles would be used if the benefits did not outweigh the cost of creating another legal person that is required to pay taxes on its net worth.

With all wealth taxed at the same small flat rate, there would be little incentive to maintain assets offshore for tax reasons. A significant amount of assets that are now offshore would return to the country of domicile of the persons in control of the funds since return of these assets to the US would reduce political risk, increase investment utility, and make it easier for owners of wealth to maintain actual control over their assets.

"Evaluation Difficulties" Problem

Some people have objected that a tax upon net worth is too complicated for the taxpayer or the taxing authority to calculate. How does one establish the value of real estate on a particular date? What about good will of a business? What is the value of a note secured by a deed of trust at 6% interest? Fairness depends upon some sort of consistency in valuation technique, doesn't it?

Certainly, valuation issues can be complex. But they are no more difficult than the same problems we face with today's tax system. The estate tax system is one that requires the valuation of assets and the calculation of net worth. And there are many, many existing Treasury Regulations that deal with issues of valuation of virtually every asset known in virtually every circumstance.

Nor is it so easy to define "taxable income" of various types in various circumstances. That's why so many Treasury Regulations and Revenue Rulings are necessary to build a body of law that can be followed on these issues. Yet we can deal with this complexity.

Complexity of the law would still be required under the Fair Tax System, but only with respect to the valuation of assets and liabilities. We could load the volumes and volumes of enacted law and regulations, the even more of revenue rulings and treatises devoted solely to the taxation of income, sales, real property, etc. and the still more that are devoted to taxes by other names such as car registration fees, tolls, park fees, fishing license fees, sin taxes, to name just a few, and dump them into a recycling plant. The sheer volume of pulp could supply all the newsprint needed in the United States for the next fifty years and substantially reduce deforestation.

How would this system work? It would work largely as it does today. Ours is a system that has always been dependent upon voluntary tax compliance.

In the first instance, it would be for the taxpayer to value his or her assets and after subtracting liabilities arrive at net worth. Most valuation issues are simple. Most people have only small bank accounts and perhaps some liquid or semiliquid retirement investment accounts. Those that have real estate mostly own a single-family residence. And most of them have a pretty good idea of the value of their house. The complex issues of valuation are most important when it comes to people or institutions of moderate to substantial wealth.

There are market driven forces which discourage the underreporting of net worth, particularly in the preparation of balance sheets prepared for business or investment purposes and those provided to financial institutions for credit purposes to attract new capital or to public agencies to maximize value of publicly traded securities. Especially with the advent of the computerization of the world, such reporting can be compared against tax returns to ferret out tax cheating through deliberate undervaluation for tax purposes. With appropriate criminal and civil penalties, especially given the uniformly low level of taxation expressed as a percentage of wealth, tax cheating can further be discouraged. It simply won't be worth the risk.

Different assets bring different valuation problems along with them. The Internal Revenue Service and state tax authorities already have regulations which deal with the valuation of virtually every type of asset. Following valuation prescriptions of Treasury Regulations and Revenue Rulings is no more difficult in the context of valuation than it is in any other area of taxation. Before we get off the target, and since the problem may not be obvious to all, let's discuss a simple example.

If a three-year-old note evidencing a $100,000 debt which is payable interest only for ten years at 5% interest is sold, a buyer will be willing to pay one price or another based upon various factors. Therefore, the value of the note at any time will differ depending upon these factors. If it is adequately secured by a lien on real property, then it is less risky than an unsecured note. If it is secured by a first lien, it is less risky than if secured by a second lien. If market interest rates are at 5%, and the risk is low, it will be worth pretty much its face value. If market interest rates are at 10%, this will reduce the value of the asset accordingly.

So you see, although some assets are more difficult to value than others, all assets can be valued with a sufficient degree of accuracy.

The auditing function of the Internal Revenue Service will come into play largely as it does now. It will monitor returns filed and pursue those taxpayers that don't file returns. It will review tax returns and audit a few returns each year at random, looking for accuracy of reporting and valuation. It will flag some returns for audit when the nature of assets reported makes it easy to misstate the value of substantial assets or when valuation of assets differs widely from year to year. When the IRS disagrees with a valuation by the taxpayer, it will challenge valuation.

CHAPTER 7

✧ ✧ ✧

The Structural Prescription

Revenue Sharing with the States and Local Governments

The most efficient way to assess and collect taxes under the Fair Tax System is through one central taxing authority. Collect taxes at the national level and then distribute revenue back to the states to fund state and local government programs.

The states would lobby Washington for an equitable distribution of funds predicated upon population and consideration of those other legitimate needs of the state and local governments unrelated to population.

Since the House of Representatives has, according to the US Constitution, the power of the purse (all funding bills must originate in the House), it could initially make the required allocations in the same way it passes a budget today. Each state is represented in the House roughly according to population. It would seem, therefore, the ideal body in which the "horse trading" would initially occur. Then the bill would move to the Senate, in which every state has equal representation. The version passed in the Senate might be a bit different, of course. Like any bill, differences would be reconciled in conference and returned to both houses for ratification.

The executive branches of our governments are given the task of administering and implementing the decisions of the legislatures respecting budgeting. Because the possibility of executive veto exists under the systems in the United States, the executive branch is also involved in proposing all sorts of legislative policy and goals, including with respect to budgeting.

Departments of the executive branches are run by all sorts of people who are nominated by the executive and confirmed, in the case of the federal government, by the Senate. For example, the Senate and the president are involved in determining who will be Secretary of the Treasury, Secretary of the Department of Commerce, Attorney General of the United States, Ambassador to the United Nations, etc. Each of these bureaucracies has an important budgeting role, submitting its budget request and analysis of its budget needs with respect to the work of each executive department. The power of the House over the budget process keeps these executive branches of the government responsive to legislative policy decisions reflected in laws.

The third branch of government in the American Constitutional system, the Judiciary, also has its budgetary requirements and submits its input to the legislature as well.

Right now, the federal government distributes a substantial part of the taxes collected at the federal level to the states and local governments through all sorts of programs and mechanisms. State houses already approach the Congress regularly and lobby both through their governors, through paid lobbyists, and through their federal representatives in the Congress and the Senate for their just allocation of this revenue sharing.

Ultimately the budget decisions of the Congress reflect the "working out" of all competing interests.

The states, too, already go through similar processes as the federal government. It would be a relatively simple matter for them to prepare similar budget, program and policy information for submittal to Washington, both to the House Budget Office and the president, making the case for their budgetary needs and desires.

Because the House's budget will need to consider and balance many competing interests, the states will be well advised to consider their programs not only in terms of local concerns but also in context of benefits to national interests. The better it can make a case in the latter context, the more successful will be its appeal to legislators from other states whose support will be needed to fully fund the individual state's budgetary desires.

But even local budgetary concerns can be effectively lobbied in the normal horse trading tradition of the legislature.

Independent Taxation by State and Local Governments

In many cases, the states could receive its entire budget from redistribution of tax revenues collected by the federal government. However, given our federal system, it is apparent that many if not most states will elect to tax, and collect taxes, themselves.

The states that have income tax laws now generally mimic the federal income tax as to details such as definitions of taxable income, taxable events, deductibility of expenses, etc. for ease of understanding and compliance by its citizens.

Compared to income tax, it would be easy for any state to mimic the federal fair tax system and the laws and regulations implementing it.

If the federal government taxed wealth at 2%, a state government could require businesses doing business in the state, and/or residents of that state, to pay taxes directly to the state, at, say .2%. But, as in most things political, the devil is in the details of who would be subject to state tax and how much to tax. Let's take a look at how one version of this might work.

Once the allocation of federal revenue sharing was determined in any one year for the next year, state and local governments could plan their programs and expenditures accordingly. They would have the option of living within the means afforded by the process of taxation of wealth at the federal level and the reallocation of resources to the states through the legislative process in the House of Representatives, or not.

Of course, under the Constitution of the United States, the power to tax is a concurrent power, meaning both the state and the federal governments have the power to tax. Therefore, each state could use its power to tax to supplement revenues to that state as it saw fit and probably would, at least from time to time and in modest amounts.

Let's consider the issues from the perspective of the state as a taxing authority, understanding that from the point of view of every county, parish, or municipality, the issues would be the same but on a smaller scale.

Domiciliaries

The concept of domicile is well established in the law. It is where the individual's principal residence is located. One can have many residences, but only one domicile. One is domiciled in the place in which he or she maintains a primary residence. It is largely a matter of intention. Since Roman law, one's domicile remains until a new domicile is established. The place in which one registers to vote is a frequent test.

If the states continued to tax separately in the Fair Tax System, they would likely tax their domiciliaries at rates different from those rates adopted by other states. Therefore, the relative tax burden would become, especially for people of significant wealth, a key consideration of where to call home. All things being equal, they would tend to gravitate to the lowest tax state in which to maintain a principal residence. This fact would be a strong incentive to states to keep separate taxes low.

Assets Maintained in the State,
County, or Local Government

Of course, each state could and should tax any assets maintained in that state regardless of the domiciliary state of the owner since those assets are being protected and preserved by that state's police, fire service, courts, etc.

Real estate, the asset that can't be moved, would be taxed in the state in which it was located.

Respecting other hard assets such as cars, private jets, yachts, etc., it might be more difficult to determine which state has the right to tax. If an individual domiciled in California, for instance, has assets warehoused in Nevada, Nevada may claim to have the right to collect tax on those assets kept there.

For instance, consider a California domiciliary that keeps a $40,000 speed boat docked in a marina on Lake Havasu. Since the asset is transportable personal property of the California resident, California may require its value to be included in the net taxable estate of its resident. But since Nevada is maintaining the political and social infrastructure which protects the asset, Nevada may require it to be included in assets taxable under Nevada law. Interstate compacts may be negotiated to deal with conflicts to ameliorate their harsh effects.

More Complex Problems—Some Ideas

Stock brokerage accounts, bank accounts, pension accounts, all accounts, should be taxed in the state in which the beneficial owner resides.

Most publicly traded securities are owned in the house name enabling greater liquidity of assets. In other words, if one owns stock in a Merrill Lynch account, the account owner beneficially owns the stock, but the stock is issued and held in the name of Merrill Lynch. But it matters not where the actual securities are housed. The brokerage will have a liability offsetting the asset, and therefore no net worth attributable to the existence of the account. Only the beneficial owner will be taxed on its value. And the value of the account then should be allocated to the customer on a day fixed for valuation.

As to the mechanics of tax payment, these financial accounts present at least two possibilities. One is to require reporting by the brokerage of the identity of the beneficial owners of the assets in the account on a date certain and the value of the account. The other is to require the brokerage to pay the tax and then to deduct the cost of the tax from the balance in the account.

In the latter case, the identity of the owner would not need to be reported for tax purposes. Payment by the brokerage provides for ease of collection to the customer's domiciliary state and the IRS. Reporting provides the benefit of a paper trail back to the beneficial owner. Direct payment by the brokerage provides a degree of privacy for the beneficial owner, which for many people may be considered a desirable effect. So long as the assets remain in an account in which an institution is paying the tax, the identity of the beneficial owner is not information needed by a taxing entity. And given the value of the right to privacy, this may be a deciding factor.

The same mechanics worked out for securities brokers such as Merrill Lynch or the Fidelity Fund could be applied to other account holding institutions such as banks.

Real estate could be taxed to the legal owner or beneficial owner based upon the net equity in the property determined by the formula, fair market value of the property less the debt secured by the property. Since the mortgage or trust deed document that creates the lien advises as to the maximum size of the debt secured, the holder of the note would have every incentive to report the balance of the loan on the valuation date to not be taxed on any portion of the debt that has been paid down. The property owner's liability then would be predicated on the market value of the property less the balance of the loans which the property secures on the valuation date.

Mortgage holders utilizing local property to secure a debt own an asset—i.e., the note and security interest—and can be required to pay a tax to the state in which the property is situated even if the lender is not resident of that state because the political and social institutions of that state are necessary to afford the owner of the note the security interest and to protect the value of the security, i.e., the property and its improvements.

In all such cases in which more than one state has a legitimate claim to tax a single asset, again, some kind of tax compact between states can be worked out so as not to destroy some the fairness of the Fair Tax System. Tax treaties which exist between nation states provide examples of workable solutions, such as providing the tax payer in the higher tax state a credit for the tax paid in the lower tax state.

Corporations and Other Business Entities

Corporations and other business entities are chartered by the states. When an entity is chartered in one state and is doing business in another state, it must file with the state in which it is doing business.

The overall value of publicly traded companies is easy enough since the net value of the company is the collective value of the various classes of equity shares in the company owned. The question remains, how to determine what percentage of the value of the company is fairly taxed by a single state that opts to tax separately.

One might look at the proportion of the equity owned by entities domiciled in the state and apply that percentage against the net value of all equity shares. This is probably not equitable, though, because many shares in publicly traded companies are owned by mutual funds and pension funds, which may be domiciled in one state that is a financial center, like New York, Chicago, or San Francisco.

Since the predicate of the Fair Tax System is to pay taxes in direct proportion to the taxpayers' benefit from the social and political establishment, a purer approach would be to look at various facts about the business of the company. How much of the total sales of the company take place in or from the state? What percentage of the personnel of the company resides in the state?

Based upon these factors, a percentage can be established which would be used to determine an assessment. That percentage would be applied against the net value of the company as valued by the public markets. This would enable the governments to also tax the value of good will and other intangible assets of the company. Further, in this way no more than 100% of the value of the company would be taxed at the state level as between all the states.

Of course, the company may own real estate or other hard assets within a particular state. Since the value of these assets would be included in the net value of the company as valued by the public markets, separately taxing these assets would be double counting. The net value of these assets (gross value less mortgages) could, of course, be deducted from overall company valuation and taxed solely by the state in which the asset was located.

Admittedly this stuff can get pretty complicated in actual application, which is why it would be best to work out these types of details between the states in state compacts.

These same considerations, that is the considerations applicable to the taxation of public companies, are also applicable to multistate private business entities, and the solutions vis-à-vis allocation through multistate compact would apply equally well to them.

These discussions as to specifics are meant solely to illustrate that even though the Fair Tax System is simpler than the tax systems we currently impose, it is still complicated and will require federal and state agencies to work out the details.

Factors Mitigating against States' Abuse of Taxing Authority

However the states work out the details regarding the taxation of wealth, there is a natural check upon the use of the power by states. Too aggressive use of taxation by any state will drive residents and businesses from the state.

Another benefit of a fair tax system, with taxes being determined and assessed largely at the national level, is that a free and fair market between states for population, industry, etc. will be maintained. People will not be as affected by the tax policies of the various states as to where to locate.

As of this writing, there is a minor exodus by residents of Long Island, New York, to states like North Carolina and Pennsylvania because of the lower property taxes and sales taxes in those states. The numbers of people who move to Florida and Nevada are also, at least, partially the result of the fact that these states have no income tax and have low property and sales taxes. These tax motivated relocations would all but cease under the Fair Tax System, and the character of states would gradually reflect the highest and best use to which its natural resources can be made undistorted by local tax policies.

CHAPTER 8

✧ ✧ ✧

Call to Action

In writing this book, I have only begun the process of mining the strata of economic data, digging as deeply as I am able at this time. Further economic analysis will require the assistance of the community of those economists that can see a geography greater than that which is visible by looking at the minutiae within the current landscape. George Bernard Shaw once wrote, "Some men see things as they are and say, 'Why?' I dream of things that never were and say, 'Why not?'" In that spirit, I invite those with a deeper education in and understanding of economics to contribute to the ideas expressed in this book.

Interestingly, in my endeavors to find the facts from the statistics available, I found that those statistics that are readily available seem to be compiled more to obscure the truth of the nature and extent of the wealth divide in this country than to elucidate it.

I have endeavored to present a rationale based on history, a "back to the future" argument, if you will. I have argued from the perspective of the moral and ethical principles found in the holy scripture of the great religions, though I am no biblical scholar. The fairness imperative proposed has been justified to some extent under social contract theory. I have revealed my thoughts tied to the broad outline of the arguments for and against, and a general understanding of the structural changes to our political and economic systems that would be required to make the Fair Tax System a reality.

I recognize, though, that my nature is to view the world as a generalist does, one that is passionately committed to and concerned about the future of the middle class in America. We need the thoughts and contributions of specialists in the areas of religion, ethics, political science, and history, as well. I welcome such specialists into the discussion who can take their inspiration from George Bernard Shaw.

In the words of Dom Helder Camara, former Archbishop of Olinda and Recife, the poorest and least developed region of Brazil, "When we are dreaming alone it is only a dream. When we are dreaming with others, it is the beginning of reality."

So I ask you, "Can you find the courage to help foment the change required? Are you willing to actively join the 2% Solution Revolution?"

We can do this, but only as a grass roots movement, only by creating a groundswell of consciousness raising, political activity and organization. We can do this, yes, but only together.

Thankfully, today, doing this together is easier than ever because we are wired to each other. The internet and the ease of communication it creates are unprecedented in history, and our capacity to cooperate toward a common vision is greater than ever.

I invite you, the reader, to dare imagine how much better our world will be if we bring about the changes suggested in this book. Imagine how much better the world will be for you, our brothers and sisters, our children and for future generations. And when you do, get busy doing what you can do.

Talk about this book and the ideas in the book to everyone who will engage online in the virtual world and in the time and space of the real world. Give this book as a gift to your friends and loved ones that are willing to read it. Ask them what they think. Ask if they will help.

Recommend this book to your congressmen and senators, regardless of party. The principles, if understood, should appeal equally to Democrat and Republican, Progressive and Conservative. Send them a letter telling them in no uncertain terms that they must fully support the changes recommended, or in future elections, you will find a candidate to support who will. Let them know that you consider fairness in taxation the litmus test of your political support.

Talk about this book and its principles in blogs.

Send me your suggestions, ideas, questions, and comments. Refer you friends and loved ones to www.FairTaxSystem.net. Tell the deans of the various colleges and universities that they should encourage appropriate faculty to become familiar with the book and its principles and encourage discussion in their classes, in student activities, and on the internet and in conventional media. Let them know that I am available to them to speak to assemblies of college students and faculty about the critical importance of the issues and enormous transformative power of adopting the fair tax principles of this book.

Tell your pastors, rabbis, priests, imams, and leaders of community organizations and associations as well.

Keep courage by keeping in mind that although the wealthy special interests in our society may have most of the money and can buy influence, we have the votes.

By adopting "the Fair Tax System's 2% solution" as our political battle cry and by insisting that despite any other policy issues and positions, our representatives support of the "2% Solution Revolution" or lose our vote, we can change the rules of the game and level the playing field.

By taking the institutional and governmental savings from streamlining and downsizing the nonproductive costs of assessing and collecting hundreds of various taxes and fees, we can provide for the public financing of elections, reduce class size in our schools, provide higher pay to obtain more and better qualified teachers, make health care a right in America, provide free undergraduate college education to qualified students, and do so much more.

What do I want you to do? Think. Act. Insist. Join me in making this the greatest political revolution in our time.

ABOUT THE AUTHOR

As a practicing psychotherapist in Florida, Dr. Mitch has treated a large variety of patients using an eclectic mix from multiple therapeutic styles. He is married and has two adult children. Dr. Mitch has long been interested in larger social and political issues. That interest together with his observation of the "hot button" issues that spark anger in his patients and others has resulted in his view that all social "hot button" movements result from the perception of unfairness. Since all government at every level involves decisions about how to allocate public resources and how to pay for those allocations, he has studied the unfairness in how our society raises money to pay for government. This study has led to his prescription of the 2% solution.